THE
BROTHERS

PRAISE FOR ROBERT J. CONLEY

"Conley speaks with a clear Cherokee Indian voice to show how his tribe's cultural characteristics have survived centuries of abrupt change."—*The Cherokee Advocate*

"...his prose and analyses, effortlessly blending indigenous and local knowledge with the larger Western cultural canon, have undeniable charm and enduring value."—*Publishers Weekly*

"[Robert Conley is] in the ranks of N. Scott Momaday, Louise Erdrich, James Welch or W. P. Kinsella as interpreters of the many facets of the Native American experience."
—*Fort Worth Star-Telegram*

"No one weaves a tribal story quite like Robert Conley. Conley's books are entertaining, colorful, and chock-full of tribal history and culture."—Wilma P. Mankiller, former Principal Chief of the Cherokee Nation

"Robert Conley spins a fast-action tall tale salted with Western humor."—Elmer Kelton, author of *The Time It Never Rained*

"Robert Conley is one of the most underrated and overlooked writers of our time, as well as the most skilled."—Don Coldsmith, author of *Moon of Madness*

THE
BROTHERS

Robert J. Conley

SPEAKING VOLUMES, LLC
NAPLES, FLORIDA
2019

The Brothers

ISBN 978-1-64540-151-3

"They were like two enemies in love with one another."

—Fyodor Dostoyevsky, *The Brothers Karamazov*

The Family

Old Garret

Old Phillip Garret was well known in Fort Smith, Arkansas, and the surrounding area. He was a man of maybe sixty years. His hair was long and usually unkempt, totally gray. His face was puffy, especially his nose, from much drinking over a great many years. His lips were thin and blue. He was not a big man, but he was stocky, and he had a pot belly. He was almost always gruff and never pleasant. He was known to own a large mansion, one of the old ante-bellum type, and it was accompanied by several rich acres of land. He was believed to have a great deal of money, but no one knew where it was—in a bank, in tin cans buried in his back yard—it was anyone's guess.

Garret was known to have had two wives. By the first, a Cherokee woman, he had produced a child named Skylar. The mother died young, and Skylar had been taken in by the former slave, Jacob, who lived in a small shack on the Garret place. Skylar apparently almost never saw his father. Someone eventually took pity on the boy and paid to have him sent away to an eastern military school. Rumor said that he was a wild youth, given to gambling, drinking and chasing women. When the late Civil War had broken out, he had become Captain Garret in the United States Army. Little was known of him after that.

Old Garret remarried after his first wife's death, and by his second wife he had two more sons. Their names were Keenan and Wesley. Their lives were much like Skylar's had been. They were each raised for their early years by old Jacob and then sent away to school by someone. Keenan became an intellectual who wrote articles on theological subjects and became fairly well-to-do and somewhat famous for it, although he was said to be an atheist. His younger brother, Wesley, went to a religious school and became very devout.

Old Garret seldom thought about his sons. They were out of sight and out of mind. What was on his mind was women. Well, one woman in particular. He had seen a young and beautiful Cherokee woman in Fort Smith and was making inquiries about her. Her name was Adaline, and she lived alone somewhere in Fort Smith. Phillip Garret had decided that Adaline should be his next wife. He was tired of living alone with no one to torment besides his former slave Jacob. Well, there was another.

Also living on the Garret place in another old shack was a second black servant. This one was known only as the Stinker. He had been the son of a poor woman who wandered the streets of Fort Smith begging for pennies or for food. After she had given birth to her son, she died, and Jacob had taken the child in to raise. Stinker was treated very badly by old Garret, almost as if he had been a slave.

Skylar, The Oldest

Skylar knew from an early age that he was a Cherokee, in spite of the way he had been raised, and he carried with him always a great deal of pride in that fact. He also knew, from a cousin of his mother, a Mister Gray Mouse, that his mother had possessed a deal of money and the big house which old Phillip now called his. Skylar had written to Phillip now and then asking for money, and Phillip had sent him small amounts, but Phillip always swore that Skylar's mother had owned nothing, and that the house and all of the money was his and his alone. Skylar harbored a deep resentment because of that.

Skylar was a tall and darkly handsome man. He was a few years short of thirty, and he sported a small mustache, which curled downward on the ends. And though he was no longer in the army, he always dressed immaculately in a fine suit and a silken shirt. He wore tall highly polished black boots with his trousers tucked inside them. Under his vest, he wore two Colts .45 in holsters that held them high, above his waist with the handles reversed, so that in order to pull them out, Skylar had to perform what is known as a cross-draw. He did so quickly, and his aim was good. He was known to have killed two men in duels.

Skylar had spent all the money he had from his service career and from his father, and he decided that he would go home, if he could call it that, to Fort Smith to confront his father regarding his inheritance. His plan was to claim his house and his money and drive the old man out, at least into one of the many small shacks that stood around the place. They had most likely been built originally for slave quarters. Skylar thought that would be good enough for the old profligate Phillip Garret.

When he reached Fort Smith, Skylar went immediately on the rounds of the local taverns. He made some acquaintances who managed to get him an invitation to a party at the home of a woman famous for her great parties. Her guests were always prominent people from around the area. Skylar went to the party and met her. Her name was Katherine Durwood, and Skylar fell immediately in love with her. He courted her for a while and then proposed marriage. She accepted. Then as his fate always had it, he met another woman. A Cherokee woman named Adaline, she was beautiful, and Skylar began pursuing her.

Keenan, The Intellectual

Two or three years younger than his brother Skylar, Keenan had few memories of the Garret house and Fort Smith. He remembered old Jacob almost as his father though, and he had loving memories of the old black man. Beyond that, his memories were of school. He had loved his life at school, although he made few friends. He spent his spare time with various professors, discussing ideas, debating, and generally improving his mind. Even so, he wouldn't really call any of them his friends. They were acquaintances, useful acquaintances to be sure, but nonetheless, mere acquaintances.

Keenan had made a thorough study of the Bible and decided early on that it was only a good book, no more than that. He did not believe in the miracles, in the immaculate conception, in the raising from the dead, and he believed that if Christ was really nailed to the cross, he had died there and that was that. In short, he became an atheist at an early age. Upon his graduation, he began writing scholarly articles and selling them to various periodicals, and he developed quite a reputation.

He had suddenly astonished everyone in Fort Smith who was even acquainted with old Phillip Garret by showing up at the Garret house unannounced and staying there. Old Phillip was initially worried that another of his sons would be asking him for money, but such was not the case. Keenan simply wanted to stay there in the house. He and Phillip developed the habit of sitting around the dining table for hours drinking brandy.

Wesley, The Good

Wesley was the strangest of them all. He was shy and quiet, very studious, but all of his studies were of the Bible. He read the Bible over and over, and he read books and articles written about the Bible. He was astonished at first when he ran across articles in respectable journals on theological subjects written by his brother, but then he became very proud of his brother. He knew next to nothing about his oldest brother, Skylar. He was a captain in the army. That was all.

When Wesley was about a year away from graduation, a distinguished gentleman visited the university. His name was Reverend Wright, and he delivered guest lectures and a guest sermon. Wesley was enthralled. He was captivated by this remarkable man. Wright seemed to be miles above all of the professors Wesley had ever had in school. The man was brilliant. He knew more than any other ten men Wesley had ever known. When he learned that Reverend Wright was going back to his mission at Fort Smith, Wesley determined to follow him. He dropped out of all his classes and arranged transportation. If they refused to allow him to stay at the mission, he could resort to his father's house.

The Fourth Brother

We mustn't neglect the Stinker. He was a man a year or so younger than Skylar. He was very dark, almost black. Of medium height and fair features, he was never dressed at all. He owned only overalls, which he wore with no other stitch of clothing. He owned no shoes. He referred to himself and to his mother as niggers. He knew no other word to describe either of them. He had lately heard the rumors that old Phillip Garret had fathered him on a poor, wandering black woman in Fort Smith. But Garret had never married the woman. She had died leaving him a small baby, and Jacob had taken him in to raise. Stinker did not like Garret, but he had nowhere to go. The shack at the Garret place was the only home he had ever known. And he did not know anything or have the skills necessary to go out looking for something else.

Stinker was a bastard. He knew that word for everyone used it to describe him. He did not know much else except for the chores that were assigned him. He had never been to school, and he did not care. Why should he? Garret fed him and gave him a shack to live in. What more did he need? Perhaps a name other than Stinker. He was not acknowledged as a son of Garret. He was not allowed to use the name. Stinker was trapped. Although slavery had been outlawed, old Garret knew how to keep at least two slaves, and he was one of them. There was nothing he could do about it.

The Gathering

♦ ♦ ♦

Jacob took the buggy around to the front door of the big plantation home and secured the horse to the hitch rail there. He hurried up onto the porch, to the front door, opened the door and called out, "Mister Phil. Mister Phil, the buggy's a waiting. They'll all be waiting for you at the mission."

"I know. I know, you black bastard. I'm coming," Phillip Garret said. Garret strode through the huge and nearly empty living room of the old mansion, dressed in his very best. He even astonished old Jacob with his appearance. His tall, black riding boots were polished to a high sheen. That, of course, was no surprise to Jacob, as he had done the polishing. But the rest of the outfit was what amazed the old former slave. It must have been in moth balls since the beginning of time. The old master did look presentable, but Jacob smelled the moth balls when Phil walked close by him. Old Garret stomped past Jacob and on out to the waiting buggy, where he got into the back seat.

Jacob shut the front door to the house and then unhitched the horse. He got himself into the driver's seat and took up the reins. He was holding a buggy whip in his right hand. He gave a flick of the reins, clicked his tongue, and snapped the whip just above the horse's head. The buggy started with a lurch. "Get her moving, Jacob," growled old Phil. "We mustn't be late. We'd keep them waiting for us at the church, by God."

"No sir. We don't want to keep them waiting, sir," said Jacob. They did not have far to go, as the mission and the Garret house both were west of Fort Smith a few miles, and they were just about six miles from one another. Old Phillip carried his top hat in his lap to keep from losing it in the wind, and his white hair, unruly in the best of conditions, was blowing wild. He had the appearance of an old fur trapper dressed up for a wedding, or perhaps a funeral.

"Your whole family going to be there, Mr. Phil, ain't it?"

"That's the plan, Jacob," Garret said, and he did not say it out loud, but his thoughts continued, "We might just as well call it your family as mine."

He heard the sounds of a horse's hooves coming up beside him as they moved along, and although he did not think it dignified, he turned his head to see who it might be. Jacob did the same, and the old black man was the first one to speak. With a broad grin on his face, he said, "Good evening, Mr. Keenan."

"Hello, Jacob," answered Keenan Garret, tipping his hat as he rode up alongside the buggy and slowed his mount so as not to pass them by, "Father."

"How are you, my sweet boy," said the old man. "At least we two will be on time."

Keenan pulled a watch out of his pocket and glanced at it. "We have plenty of time, Father," he said. "'Come what come may, time and the hour runs through the roughest day.'"

"Quoting the Bible again, huh?"

"Shakespeare, Father. It was Shakespeare. From *Macbeth*."

"Ha ha," laughed old Garret. "I knew it. Fooled you, didn't I? Of course I've read *Macbeth*."

They rode on for another half-mile in silence, and then Phil said, "I read Shakespeare, you know. Of course I do, and the Bible, too. But I read nothing else. Not a Goddamned thing else."

They rode on until they arrived at the mission. They rode past the outbuildings right up to the front door of the main building, where they were met by a young man, an Indian boy, who took their horses. He tied them to the hitch rail and gestured toward the front door. "Right in here," he said.

"Reverend Wright is waiting for you. Along with Wesley."

Phillip and his son Keenan went into the mission building. They both stopped and looked around. Neither had been inside the mission before. They were in a huge and open room.

One section held rows of pews facing a podium. There were pictures of Jesus on the walls, and one corner of the room was decorated like a small living room, with

11

a couch and a few chairs and one low table in front of the couch.

Reverend Wright, an elderly gentleman, and a young man, Wesley Garret, stood up from the couch and moved toward the two other Garrets. Jacob had been left outside with the horses.

"Welcome, friends," said Wright, extending his hand for old Garret to shake.

"How do you do, your reverendship," said Garret.

Wesley cringed, but he covered it up well enough. He nodded respectfully to old Phillip Garret, and said, "Good evening, Father."

"How do you do, my boy," said Phil. "Are you getting enough to eat in this place?"

"Of course, Father. But where is Skylar?"

"How would I know? He was informed of the time, wasn't he? Just the same as I?"

"I'm sure he'll be here," said Keenan.

"Of course he will," said Wesley.

"It is mainly on his behalf that we are here," said Keenan.

"And the kindness of Reverend Wright," said Wesley.

"Of course, of course," said Phillip. "We are all very grateful, your graciousness."

There was a knock at the door just then, and they all looked around at one another. Wright looked at Wesley. "Would you answer the door, my son?" he said.

"Of course, Reverend," said Wesley, and he walked to the front door and opened it wide.

"Is it Skylar?" said Phillip, a bit too anxiously.

"It is Mr. Gray Mouse," said Wesley, as if he were introducing a guest at a very formal ball. "My brother Skylar's mother's cousin."

"Come in and welcome, Mr. Mouse," said Reverend Wright.

"Thank you, Reverend," said Mouse, taking off his hat and handing it to Wesley, who carried it to a nearby table and placed it there very carefully. Mouse walked on over to join the others. He shook hands deliberately with each one. "Skylar has not yet arrived?" he asked.

"He'll be here," said Phillip. "If there's one thing he's good at, it's being punctual. He was an officer in the Union Army, you know, as was Mr. Mouse here."

Mouse looked over the company scowling. "You, I believe," he said, looking at Phillip, "were a Confederate."

"Loyal to Jeff Davis, Robert E. Lee and even old Stand Watie," Phillip said.

"Yet you haven't freed your slave. I saw old Jacob standing loyally out beside your buggy."

"Old Jacob is free. The Government freed him. It's not up to me. He's free to go, but he won't go. He keeps hanging on to me, so he won't starve. That's all. He wouldn't know what to do with himself if he was on his own. He needs me."

"I find it hard to believe that anyone would hang around you of his own free will," Mouse said.

"My dear son Keenan hangs around. He's living with me now after all these years. And he doesn't need to. He has his own money. He could live anywhere he wanted to. And he's an intellectual, too. He's smart. Smarter than you, you old Indian."

"Well, gentlemen," said Wright, who was himself an old man, "while we wait for the oldest son to arrive, please be seated. Make yourselves at home. And do try to be civil with one another."

Phillip settled himself quickly and comfortably at one end of the large couch and laughed out loud. "Ah, Reverend," he said, "I don't think you know what you are saying when you tell me to make myself right at home. You see, I am not only a clown, I'm a profligate. I'm rude and crude and even profane. And if I were to behave as if I were in my own home, I would even embarrass my own sons, especially my youngest, my sweet darling boy, my own Wesley, who arranged this meeting with you."

Mouse was getting nervous. He decided to change the subject. "Reverend Wright," he said, "how is your work with our young Cherokees coming along? Are you teaching our boys to wear britches?"

"The Indian children are coming along quite nicely, Mr. Mouse. Most of them can read and write in their own language, and many of them in English as well. And they have all become good Christians, I'm proud and happy to say."

A frown darkened Mouse's face. He bit his tongue. "So you teach them to renounce their own culture," he said.

"I would say, rather," said Keenan, jumping into the conversation, "that the good reverend and his staff are civilizing your little savages."

"And I say that your civilization is questionable at best," said Mouse. "White people chase thousands of Indians out of their own homes, and then they go to war amongst themselves over black people whom they have made into slaves and treat like draft animals. That is your civilization."

"People who are Christians do not always behave as Christians," said Reverend Wright. "That is one of our great failings, and one that we must constantly work against."

"If they don't behave like Christians," Mouse said, his voice growing more angry, "then they shouldn't be called Christian. They are the savages. Not we."

It was half an hour past the scheduled meeting time, and suddenly the large front door flew open, and Skylar Garret stepped into the doorway, nearly filling it. All eyes turned on him. He was a handsome man, his skin darker than the other Garrets. He was dressed neatly, almost formally, and wore two revolvers under his vest.

"There is my prodigal," said Phillip. "He's here at last."

"How like the prodigal doth he return," said Keenan, "With over-weathered ribs and ragged sails, Lean, rent, and beggared by the strumpet wind!"

"More *Macbeth*?" said Phillip.

"*The Merchant of Venice*," said Keenan.

"I stand corrected, fool that I am."

15

Skylar

♦ ♦ ♦

Skylar swung into the room, like an army officer taking charge of his troops. He forgot to shut the door behind himself, or else he just did not care. Wesley walked over and shut it. Everyone was standing by then. "Now I am surrounded by all my sons," said Phillip. "What a great feeling of warmth."

"Indeed," said Skylar. "When have you ever felt warmth for anyone?"

"That's no way to talk to your father," said Phillip. "Your own mother died when you were just a babe, and so who was left to raise you? I ask you that. Who raised you all alone?"

"I believe it was old faithful Jacob," said Skylar. "I don't even remember ever seeing you until this day."

"I was busy making a living for you."

"You were busy spending the money my mother left to me."

"And just how could your mother, an Indian, have made any money to leave you? I ask you that. Besides, I

17

have sent you money over and again during the years you were away. Do you deny that?"

"I deny nothing, but the piddling amounts you sent me over the years don't amount to what my mother left me. You know that as well as anyone."

"I kept a record. I have an accounting."

"I'd like to see that accounting. Produce it."

"Can't we speak of more pleasant things?" said Keenan. "We four are all reunited after all these years apart. Can't we get acquainted in a more pleasant fashion?"

"Yes, Skylar, my first born son. Why not? Do you know your own brothers, Keenan and Wesley? Shake hands with them now and be friends."

"My half-brothers, you mean," Skylar said. "And I never knew them either."

"It's about time we met then," said Wesley, stepping up to Skylar and extending his hand. "I'm your brother, Wesley. I'm living here in this mission with the good reverend, Mr. Wright."

Reverend Wright stepped up and put his hand out to Skylar. Skylar shook both hands, the reverend's more warmly than that of his own brother. "Reverend Wright," he said, "your reputation goes before you. I have heard great things about you. I dare say, if you were a Catholic, they would be making you a saint. The Baptists around here almost claim that for you as it is."

"Please, Mr. Garret," said Wright, "don't make so much of me. I'm a simple pastor."

"Simple is much too modest, Sir," said Wesley. "I believe my brother was correct in his assessment. That's the reason I choose to live in this mission and stay close to you."

"To receive the holy word and the blessing of the holiest of men," said Keenan. The sarcasm in his voice was clear.

"We all know that you're an atheist," said Wesley. "You don't need to parade it."

"I parade nothing," said Keenan. "Do you despise me for my beliefs?"

"No. Of course not," said Wesley. "You are my closest brother, and I love you with all my heart. I just don't like to see anyone making light of the reverend."

"My apologies, Reverend Wright," said Keenan. "I have nothing but the greatest respect for your position. I hope you'll forgive any offense I may have given to you, however inadvertently."

"Nonsense, my boy," Wright said. "No offense was given and none taken."

Skylar during all of this had paced to a near window and stood with his back to the others staring out into the yard.

"Wesley," said Keenan, "why don't you leave this mission and come live with your father and me? We'd be more like a family then. Our dear departed mother would want it that way, don't you think?"

"I love the memory of our mother more than any other thing on this earth," said Wesley, "but I love Reverend Wright and the things he can teach me. I must stay here as long as I can."

Skylar suddenly turned to face them again. "You should stay in my—in the old man's house, Wesley," he said, "with your brother, for you two have the same mother, and she was a white woman."

"Our mother died when we were very young, Skylar, as did yours," said Keenan. "Wesley and I have no stronger ties than do you and I. We're all brothers."

"Because of that nasty old man there?" said Skylar. "That thief? That's a poor link with which to forge a chain. I've even heard rumors that he fathered that servant they call Stinker. Shall we call him in and make him a fourth brother?"

"The Stinker's mother was that poor idiot girl who used to run the streets around here," said Mouse, finally injecting himself back into the conversation. "She never bathed. No one knew how she managed to get any food. She could barely speak. Everyone knows that she was Stinker's mother. When the poor girl died leaving a small child, old Jacob took the child in and raised it himself."

"So we are four brothers," said Keenan, "all raised by the same black father."

"Shut up about that," said Phillip. "You shouldn't make such vile accusations against your own father. Show some respect. For both my age and my position."

"Stinker Garret," said Skylar.

"Shut up, you," shouted Phillip.

"I must beg all of you to behave more civilly toward one another," said Reverend Wright. "I allowed you to meet here in the mission in hopes that you might work out your differences and be reconciled. You seem to be moving more toward starting a fight."

"That's Skylar's fault," said Phillip. "We all know that he has fought duels and killed men. Three or four, I believe it was."

"Two only," said Skylar.

"And they were fought over women, were they not?"

"They were."

"Judge not that ye be not judged," said the reverend.

"I have never killed over a woman," said Phillip. "Nor for any other reason except in the war."

"Would you fight and kill for Adaline?" said Skylar.

"Adaline?" said Keenan.

"That is who the old goat is currently lusting after," said Skylar.

"It's a bad thing," said Mouse, "for a father and son to be after the same woman. Especially when the son is engaged to be married to yet another woman."

"Is this true, my son?" said Wright.

"It's true. I made a terrible mistake when I asked a white woman to be my wife. Then I met Adaline."

"She is Cherokee?" asked the reverend.

"Yes, and as beautiful as time is long. I adore her."

"And have you told the other woman?" said the reverend.

"I have not. Not yet."

"Adaline doesn't want him anyway," said Phillip. "He might just as well stay with the other one. She must want him, or she would never have agreed to marry him in the first place. Adaline wants me."

"You lie, you old bastard," said Skylar.

"Here," said Wright. "I must draw the line at using foul language and calling names in the house of God."

"Reverend," said Wesley, "I am embarrassed at the behavior of my father and my brother."

"They embarrass only themselves," said Wright. "We must pray for them."

"Pray for me, too, Reverend," said Keenan. "I beg of you. I am in most need of prayer."

"You blaspheme, Keenan," said Wesley. "You don't believe."

"But I am a practical man. What if I am wrong in my beliefs? I feel as if I should cover all bets."

"You will all be in my prayers, I assure you," said Reverend Wright. "Every night."

"Even me?" said Phillip.

"You?" said Wright. "Yes. Perhaps you most of all. But now, I beg all of you to put aside your quarrels. It's meal time, and I beg you all to stay and eat with us."

"I won't have a meal at the same table with old Phillip Garret," said Mouse.

"Ha," said Phillip. "I am the one who has been offensive, and I won't allow my dear friend and sort of relative, Mouse, to miss a meal on my account. I am the one who will be leaving this company. Forgive me Reverend. I bid you all good night."

Phillip immediately left the hall. The rest of the staff of the mission along with the young students all came into the hall for their meal. A separate table was set up for the Reverend Wright and his special guests. He directed them all to their seats. Everyone was standing. Wright raised his hands and intoned a prayer for the blessing of all the company and of their food. Then all were seated.

Just at that moment, the massive front door burst open, and Phillip Garret stepped in with his arms outstretched. "Aha!" he shouted. "Just as everyone thought I was gone, here I am again. It occurred to me that I was being rude to refuse your hospitality, Reverend. Am I still welcome? Am I still invited?"

"Certainly, you're welcome," said Wright. "Here is a place for you. Please come in and sit down."

Phillip walked over to the table and took his seat. He looked over all the company as if he were just joining them for the first time. "But Mister Mouse is not pleased to see me arrive," he said. "I dare say, I have offended him in some way. Mouse, please forgive me my foolishness."

"You are nothing but an old fool," said Mouse, "and I do not forgive you for it."

"Ah, it's a heavy burden to bear," said Phillip. "My own dear brother-in-law."

"I am not your brother-in law. You are nothing to me."

A servant came around pouring coffee for everyone. Garret looked at it disapprovingly. There was a platter of bread on the table almost in front of him, and he reached for it and tore off a chunk.

He took a bite of the bread and dropped the rest of the piece onto his plate. Then he slurped some coffee. "Ah," he growled, "is this the way you eat in the mission? Hard bread and cold coffee? I eat better at home, and I drink brandy. Wesley, come home with me at once. I'll get some proper food in you. Keenan, we're leaving, now."

The old man got up to leave for the second time. This time he was followed by Keenan, but Wesley stayed in his chair with a firm look on his face. "Come along, Wesley," Phillip shouted. "I'm your father." He stomped out again, followed by Keenan but not by Wesley.

In another few moments, the meal was served. In a few more it was consumed. Reverend Wright excused himself to go to bed. He was old and somewhat ill. Wesley went with him, and Mouse and all the rest excused themselves and took their leaves.

Skylar stomped rudely out of the building. He got his horse by the reins and stood by the porch as Mouse walked by. Skylar said, "How can such a man be allowed to live? I should kill him."

"He's not worth a killing," said Mouse. "Don't dirty your hands."

Wesley helped Reverend Wright out of his clothes, into his nightshirt and into bed. As the old man settled back into his pillow, he heaved a long and heavy sigh. "Wesley, my son," he said. "I love you, and I've been happy with you living here, but it's time for you to go now."

"To go?" said Wesley. "But why? And where?"

"Your place is with your brothers—and your father."

Back at the Garret House a small, black man sat alone in the dining room at a big table. He was wearing a pair of overalls and nothing more. His feet were bare. He had a bottle of brandy on the table before him and a glass which he had just drained. He picked up the bottle and poured the glass full again.

He loved being in the big house alone, when everyone else was gone. He had the run of the house, and he enjoyed himself, drinking the master's brandy, sitting in the master's chair. He hoped they would not return until it was way late into the night. As he drank the brandy, he thought about the meeting over at the mission. All of the Garrets were supposed to be there. Old Phillip, his sons Wesley and Keenan, and the wanderer, the notorious Skylar. The father and his three sons. Three. Ha. A regular family reunion.

Out loud, brave because he was alone in the house, he cursed them all, consigned them all to hell. If old Phillip, the evil old son of a bitch, knew what he was doing, he would beat him. He knew that, but Phillip would not find out. Phillip was almost always too drunk to notice the level of brandy in his bottle, so he would drink as much as he liked while they were all away. He would enjoy himself just as if it were his own birthright.

The Sins of the Father

♦ ♦ ♦

Wesley had a horse in the stable, so he packed up his few belongings, slowly and reluctantly, wondering why the Reverend Wright was being so unreasonable with him, and then he carried the bag slowly out to the stable where he saddled his horse. He stood there beside his mount for a few moments, feeling like a lost soul. At last he mounted and tied the grip to the saddle horn. He urged the horse forward, but he rode slowly, as if he had until the end of the world to get to where he was going.

Up ahead at a small stream, Phillip ordered Jacob to stop in the low water to allow the horse to drink. Keenan stopped his horse in the stream as well. "I wish it was so easy for us to get a drink of brandy," Phillip said. "I'd have stayed at the mission for dinner, except they had no brandy. God damned cheap skate God-talking bastards."

"Now, Father," said Keenan, "they don't curse you for what you drink in your house, and you shouldn't curse them for what they have to drink in theirs."

"But it isn't even their own damned house," said Phillip, "is it? Don't they call it God's house?"

27

Keenan laughed. "Yes. You're right, of course. Have we paused long enough here?"

"No. Wait. I hear a rider coming. Do you have your pistol?" He drew one of his own out from under his great coat and cocked it.

"No, Father. I don't carry one. 'He who lives by the sword shall die by the sword.'"

"And he who lives by the gun shall last longer than the other fellow."

"Perhaps."

The rider behind them came closer, though he was moving at a very slow pace. "It's Mister Wesley," said Jacob. "For God's sake, Mister Phillip, don't go to shooting. It's your own son."

"Wesley," Keenan called. "Come on. Catch up with us."

Phillip eased the hammer down on his revolver and tucked it back under his coat. He laughed out loud. "Ah, Wesley, my boy. Come up beside me here. No. On this side. Your brother is riding on that side. That's it. So you decided to obey me after all."

"No, Father, I did not."

"What?"

"Reverend Wright turned me out. He said my place was with you and my brothers."

"Well, then, he showed some good sense after all. I liked him. I thought he was a good and a holy man. Don't you agree, Keenan? I know that Wesley agrees. Wesley believes that the man has actual angel's wings on his back."

"Father," said Wesley, "you exaggerate."

"Always, of course. It's in my nature. But you can't obey your reverend completely, you know, not if he said you belong with your brothers. Skylar, of course, will not live with me. He must stay over in the damned Cherokee Nation at a shack in Webber's Falls, with all the Indians. But maybe it doesn't matter anyhow. He's only your half brother."

"He won't stay over there for long at a time," said Keenan. "It's much too far away from his beloved Adaline."

"Don't speak of her in the same breath as that swine your brother," said Phillip. "She's going to be your step mother."

"Father," said Wesley, "don't you think it's unseemly for you to be pursuing a woman of her age? You're old enough to be her father—her grandfather."

"I am not. I'm not so old. I was a young man when I begot you children."

"'. . .and I am declined into the vale of years, yet that's not much,'" said Keenan.

"God damned Shakespeare again," said Phillip.

"Yes."

"*Macbeth* again?"

"*Othello*."

"That's the one about the nigger and the white girl, isn't it?"

"If you want to put it that way."

"How else would you put it? He got himself killed, too. Just as he deserved."

"He didn't get himself killed, Father, he killed himself out of remorse."

"Remember the old story about the Cherokee, Shoe Boots. He married his dead wife's nigger slave, and they had kids. The Cherokees should have killed him, and put the kids in flour sacks with rocks and thrown them in the river."

"You're talking like a savage now," said Keenan.

"And you're talking like a preacher. That's a strange way for an intellectual atheist to talk."

"We're a strange family," said Wesley.

"If you think we're strange, just wait until we have Skylar with us," Keenan said.

"Skylar is not family," said Phillip. "His mother was a savage."

"Why did you marry her, Father, if you feel that way about her?" said Keenan.

"I thought she had land," said Phillip. "She deceived me. God damn her, and I'm sure that he has deceived me as well."

"I don't believe that God will damn people who were not raised in his church," said Wesley. "He won't punish people for what they don't know."

"She was married to me," said Phillip. "She can't plead ignorance."

"I think perhaps she can more easily plead ignorance after living with you," Wesley said.

"You heard the preacher," said Phillip. "Most of the Cherokees today are Baptists."

"Was Skylar's mother a Baptist?" Wesley asked.

"She was a goddamned heathen."

"I rest my case."

When they reached the Garret home. Jacob put the horse and buggy away and then went to his own cottage to fix himself a modest meal. He had mixed feelings, for he was happy to see the two white boys he had raised, but he felt tortured to watch them fighting with their father.

Phillip insisted that his two sons accompany him to his study, where he broke out three glasses and a bottle of brandy. He poured three glasses and gave one to each of the two sons. Then he picked up his glass and held it up for a toast. "To having all the family home together again," he said, and he downed his drink, then poured himself another. Keenan took a sip of his own drink, and Wesley merely touched his lips to his glass.

"Drink up, boys. Drink up," said Phillip, reaching for the bottle. Keenan turned up his glass and finished off the drink. Phillip refilled the glass. "That's the way. Come on, Wesley. Come on, boy."

"I, um, I'm unused to strong drink, Father."

"Well, then, get used to it," Phillip said. "Drink up."

Wesley but touched the brandy to his lips once more. Phillip drained his glass again and poured it full another time.

"Father," said Wesley, "what Skylar said about Stinker—was it true? Or how did such a vile rumor get started?"

"The vile rumor got started when I made her pregnant," said Phillip.

"But how did it happen?"

31

"Ha. The usual way. No immaculate conception. Not in this house."

"But how could you—I mean, what was she?"

"She was a freed person, I think," said Phillip. "Part white, I believe, and perhaps part Indian, I don't know, but certainly most part black. A negress she was, and about half crazy. Everyone said so anyhow. She wandered the streets begging for food or money. My first wife was dead, and the negress came by the house begging. I let her in and gave her a few coins, and then I had my way with her. What's wrong with that?"

"It's absolutely sinful, Father," said Wesley.

"It's not your place to speak to your father like that."

"And nine months later," said Keenan, "along came a surprise. A little stinky one."

"Stinky is as stinky does," said Phillip. "Then one day she was found dead down by the river. It seemed she had a place down there where she had been staying with the brat. It's remarkable that he survived. Jacob took the wretched babe in and raised him."

"So this Stinky is my elder brother," said Keenan.

"As is the other one," said Phillip. "That damned Skylar."

"Father," said Keenan, "what is the original source of all this trouble between you and Skylar? It's not just this Adaline, is it?"

"I already had my eye on Adaline before Skylar even showed his face in Fort Smith. He saw her and wanted her, and I think he even wanted her more than ever when he discovered that I was pursuing her for marriage. He's a horrible son. But no. That was not the origin of our troubles. He's a wild one, he is. For years I never saw him, but he wrote me letters begging for money. He claimed that I was holding money his mother left him, and so I sent him money from time to time, and so he spent it on drink and gambling and on women. When he found Adaline and started pursuing her, in spite of me, he wanted his money, all of it, to help him in his pursuit. I refused him."

"You said that you have a reckoning of all the money you've paid him," said Keenan. "Is that true?"

"Of course, it's true, and what it shows is that I do not owe him any money. Instead, he is in debt to me."

"Perhaps if I were to talk with him," Keenan began, but he was interrupted by his father.

"Damn him," said Phillip. "I need no go-betweens to talk for me to my own son. Besides, there's nothing to talk about. He'll not get another penny from me."

Phillip poured himself another brandy, and, even though Keenan's glass was not empty, Phillip poured it full again. They drank. Even Wesley took a small sip of his drink. Then Wesley said, "What about this other woman? The one that Skylar is said to be engaged to marry?"

"Oh, Katharine? She's a rare beauty, she is. A white woman, too. And rich, I think. I'm a fool for not pursuing her instead of another savage. Skylar begged her for her hand in marriage, and she accepted. Then he met Adaline."

"How does Skylar hope to get himself out of this mess he has created?" said Wesley.

"My impression of our older brother," said Keenan, "is that such things don't bother him. He is guided only by his appetite. Nothing else gets in his way. This Katharine is most fortunate that he revealed his true nature before they were wed. Most fortunate. Father, have you met the woman?"

"Never," said the old man. "I understand that she owns a more than modest home on the other side of the city where she entertains guests of political importance."

"So Skylar has a fiancée who is a wealthy white woman with important friends in high places, and he insists on pursuing this Cherokee girl who is a nobody," said Keenan.

"She's the most beautiful nobody I've ever seen," said Phillip.

Ignoring his father's latest comment, Keenan said, "What is wrong with our brother?"

"I can think of nothing that's right with him, the son of a bitch," said Phillip.

"Father!" said Wesley.

"I should have drowned him when he was born. The world would be a better place if I had."

"I've had quite enough to drink," said Wesley, "and I fear I've already had too much conversation. I need to go to bed."

"Jacob can show you where to go," said Phillip. "It's a long while since you've been here. Do you recall the way to Jacob's cabin?"

"Yes. Of course," said Wesley. "Good night to you both." He turned and walked out of the room. Phillip turned immediately to Keenan.

"Do you intend to leave me as well?"

"No, Father, not unless you're ready to retire."

"Well, I'm not. I mean to get drunk, and I want company." He poured his glass full once more.

"That sounds jolly to me," said Keenan. "I'll be glad to keep you company." He held out his glass for Phillip to fill.

Wesley found his way to bed, but he did not sleep. He lay awake in bed thinking over the events of the day and evaluating his new acquaintance with his family. He wondered what he had done to be deserving of such a family. Could it be that the sins of the father were actually visited on the children?

It almost seemed so. He thought about the vile behavior of his father, the wild and excessive behavior of his brother Skylar and the casual atheism of his brother Keenan. He did not think of himself as a fanatical Christian. He only tried to be a good man, and he did admire Reverend Wright very much.

Wright was a good man, perhaps the best man he had ever known in his life, and he was sad that the reverend had sent him out into the world. He was afraid that Wright was not long for this realm, and he wanted desperately to spend as much time as he could with the old man while he was still around.

He tried to evaluate his own feelings. He was not worried for the souls of his family. He was not even sure that he believed in the rewards of Heaven and Hell. There might well be some sort of reward in the afterlife, but not eternal hymn singing for the good and eternal flames for the bad. He couldn't believe that. There were too many people who were neither good enough nor bad enough to be consigned to either place.

And what about himself? Was he good enough for Heaven? He could not think himself worthy, nor could he imagine being in such a place for eternity. To praise God eternally? That would be a boring existence. A boring existence indeed.

And then he wondered about the Stinker. So he had three brothers. Not just two. He wanted to meet the Stinker. Where was he? Did he still live with Jacob? He must have as much in common with the other brothers as they had with each other. They were all raised by the same old man, the former slave, Jacob. Wesley and Keenan had been together with Jacob but a short while before being sent away to school. Some rich benefactor, a man of the church, perhaps, had taken pity on them and paid their expenses, and they had been sent to different schools. Both of them back east. Actually all three for Skylar too had been sent away to school. They had not seen each other again until just recently. As he finally drifted off to sleep, Wesley was thinking how he would like to meet the Stinker.

The Stinker

♦ ♦ ♦

It was five days later around nine o'clock in the morning when Wesley, just barely awake, heard a knock on his door. He got out of bed and quickly pulled on his trousers. Then he walked to the door and opened it. There was a young man standing there. He wore a subservient look on his face. He was dressed in overalls, and he wore no shirt and no shoes. There was no hat on his head, and the first thing Wesley noticed about him was his hair. It was dark and had a reddish tint to it. His skin was dark, or rather darkish—and his eyes were almost black. His lips were thick and his nose had a broad and flat appearance to it, almost as if it had been flattened by a frying pan.

"Yes?" said Wesley.

"I have a note for you," the young man said.

"A note? From whom?"

"It's from a lady. She paid me to bring it to you."

37

Robert J. Conley

"Well. Let me have it then," said Wesley, holding out his hand.

The young man had been standing with both his hands inside the bib of his overalls, and he suddenly brought one out and held it toward Wesley. It held a piece of paper, folded and sealed with wax.

Wesley broke the seal and unfolded the paper. Silently, he read the note. "Dear Sir," it said, "we have not been introduced, and I beg you to forgive this forward method of contacting you. I am Katherine Durwood, and I implore you to come by my house for a visit. The subject matter of the visit is of utmost importance to me. Come as soon as you can. The messenger who brought you this note can tell you how to find me. Your humble servant, Katherine."

"Tell me," said Wesley, "who is this woman?"

"You don't know her?"

"Would I ask if I did?" Wesley wanted to say more, something like, "You fool," or "What is it that's wrong with your brain?" but instead he kept quiet.

"She's just one of the women highest on the social ladder of Fort Smith," said the messenger.

"You've been living in the mission, so I'm surprised you didn't know of her."

"Is this the woman, by any chance, that my brother Skylar is supposed to be engaged to?"

"Yes, I'm sure it is."

"Well, perhaps I should go and see her. By the way, fellow, what is your name? I am Wesley Garret."

"Yes, I know who you are. Everyone knows you. I don't have a name rightly speaking. They all just call me Stinker."

Wesley's jaw dropped, and his eyes opened wide. "Then you are my own brother. Come in. Come in and sit down."

"I don't know as how I should go into your room and sit."

"Why in the world not?"

"I'm a servant here is all. I work for old Jacob, and I'm part nigger too."

"Nonsense," said Wesley, taking him by the hand and practically dragging him into the room.

"You're a Garret. As much as any of us. Come in and let's get acquainted."

Stinker sheepishly allowed himself to be dragged into the room and seated on the edge of the bed.

"You're the next son after Skylar. Am I right in that?"

"You're right except that I'm not counted a Garret. I'm a bastard is all. I have no interest in the estate. Old Garret has said more than once that he should have put me in a flour sack with some heavy rocks and thrown me in the river when I was born."

"Our father likes to shock people," said Wesley. "He says things like that for effect, that's all. You are his son, and there are four brothers rather than just three. This is wonderful. I've been wanting to meet you. But I wish there was something I could call you other than Stinker."

"Perhaps when our father is gone, you'll see that I have a home?"

39

"A place to live and food to eat, and you won't be a servant. I promise you that."

"Oh, I don't mind being a servant. Jacob raised me that way." Then growing a little bolder and more familiar, he said, "Do you have a bottle in here?"

"Do you mean alcohol? No. I don't use it myself."

"You will, if you hang around here for long. I'll bring you one the next time I come by. Now I'd better be getting along. The old man will be looking for me."

Stinker hurried out of the room and down the hall, and Wesley watched him go. Then he went back inside his room and finished dressing. When he was done, he went downstairs and headed for the front door, but as he passed by the big table, his father saw him and yelled at him. "Hey, preacher," old Phillip called out, "where the hell are you going?"

Wesley paused on his way to the door. "I'm just going out for a little while, Father," he said.

"You just got up. You haven't eaten. Come over here to the table and sit down. Come on."

Wesley hesitated, then walked over to the table and sat at the opposite end from his father. His brother, Keenan, was also there. "I'm really not hungry," he said.

"Because the damned preachers have been starving you. They've shrunken your stomach. That's what it is. You'll eat breakfast today. Stinker. Bring more food."

Wesley was embarrassed at having his bastard brother wait on him, but he kept his mouth shut.

Soon he had a cup of coffee and some toast in front of him. He sipped the coffee and nibbled at the toast. "Where were you off to in such a hurry?" asked Phillip.

"I have to go see a lady," said Wesley.

Phillip roared with laughter. "I knew it," he said. "I knew it. You are my son after all, and there are some things that the preachers can't beat out of you, literally or figuratively. You're a toad. A horny toad."

"You mistake my meaning, Father," Wesley said. "I've been asked to pay a visit to the fiancé of my brother, and I mean to comply. That's all there is to it."

"Ohh?" The old man raised his eyebrows. "All right. I'll accept that for now. But it can easily develop into something—anything else. You're a handsome lad. Almost pretty, I'd say. But why would Skylar's intended, or once intended, I should say, why should she want to see you? She has nothing to do with you, and you have nothing to do with her. Perhaps she already has designs on you, since your brother has treated her so badly."

"Father," said Wesley, as Stinker brought him some ham and eggs, "I believe that your mind stays in the gutter. Some people have other things on their minds than drinking and whoring and gambling."

"Oh, yeah? Is that so? Well not your brother Skylar. Your precious Skylar."

"And not in this house," said Stinker, more or less under his breath.

Wesley, in spite of himself, dove into the ham and eggs. It had been too long that he had been living on gruel at the mission. The meat was delicious. It was just what he wanted, even though he had not known it. He wondered what else he might be wanting and not even know about it.

"More coffee, Stinker," said Phillip. Stinker poured the two cups full again. "And add a little brandy to it." Stinker poured some brandy into the coffee. As he poured it into Wesley's cup, he gave Wesley a smile. Wesley started to protest, but he thought again and kept quiet. Was he also craving a drink of alcohol, secretly? He did not know. Ah, he asked himself, what else?

Wesley soon excused himself and left the house. Phillip watched him go, and as soon as the big front door was shut behind Wesley, Phillip roared out, "Don't you think he'll be tupping her right soon? Eh, boys? That word is from Shakespeare too, by the way. I'm sure that you know that, Keenan, but not the Stinker there. He doesn't know anything. He can't even read or write his own name."

"Yes," said Keenan. "It's from *Othello*."

"I have no need to write my name," said Stinker. "I really don't even have one, now do I?"

The Money

♦ ♦ ♦

Wesley stood at the front door of the house of Katharine, Du—. He had forgotten her surname. He was embarrassed. He stood there trying to remember. It would not be proper for him to greet her as Katharine. He had never met the woman. He had to know her name. It was on the note she had written to him, but like a dunce, he had left it lying in his room. No. It was in his pocket. He felt for it, but just then the door opened. There the woman stood. She was radiant. Wesley's jaw dropped. At least, he thought that it had. He stared at her rudely. He felt like a crude fool.

"Hello," she said, and her voice was like a thousand diamonds being poured out onto a glass table top. "You are his brother, are you not? Skylar Garret's brother? Your name is Wesley? May I call you Wes?"

"Of course," he said. "I came, uh, because…"

He stammered. He could not speak. She was the most beautiful creature he had ever in his life seen. Her hair was golden and fell down around her shoulders in soft curls. Her breasts, which were perfectly formed, heaved with each sweet breath she drew. She must have been the model that God used to make woman. She came to his rescue. "Forgive me," she said. "I am Katharine Durwood. It was I who sent you the note. You may call me Katharine. Please. And please, come into my house."

She stepped aside, and Wesley went into the house. She followed and shut the door. She indicated a chair with a gracious sweep of her arm and said, "Please sit down, Wes."

Wesley moved to the chair and sat. He was trying desperately to overcome his nervousness, or at least, to hide it, but he knew that he was not being successful. She, on the other hand, was politely ignoring it. She rang a bell and a serving woman came into the room. "Coffee, please, Margo," she said. Then she looked at Wesley. "You do drink coffee, don't you?"

"Yes, of course I do," he said. Had she asked him if he drank turpentine, he would have said yes.

Margo left the room.

"I suppose," Katharine said, "you are wondering why I sent for you."

"That question had occurred to me," Wesley said.

"Have you heard that I'm engaged to be married—to your brother?"

"I have heard that."

"Have you also heard that he is wanting to call it off?"

"Yes, I have heard that too," said Wesley, "although until I just met you, I had no idea what kind of fool my brother was being."

44

"What do you mean?"

"I mean, I have never before seen so beautiful a woman as you are, and why any man could be engaged to you and want out of it, is a thought beyond my comprehension. I had not thought Skylar such a fool."

Katharine blushed slightly. "You are very kind, Wes," she said. "I wish your brother had more of your qualities. He seems to be more like his, uh, your father."

"Yes," said Wesley. "Skylar does favor Father." But he thought, so do I. No one knows it but I. I seem to hide it well. Perhaps all men are beasts. Underneath, all of us are alike.

"Do you think, Wes, that Skylar is really enamored with this other woman? Or is she merely a temporary distraction? I know how men are. Will he come back to me?"

"I, um, this is terribly uncomfortable."

"Don't be uncomfortable." Margo brought the coffee and poured two cups. Katherine offered cream and sugar, but Wesley took his black. Margo left the room again. "Don't be uncomfortable, Wes," said Katherine. "I'm prepared for the worst. I'm tougher than you may think. So tell me."

"I believe that Skylar intends to turn his back on his obligations. He seems to be to be very much in love with this, um, Adaline, I believe is her name. I'm sorry, Katharine."

"You needn't apologize," she said. "It's none of your doing. Thank you for being honest with me. Now you can tell him for me that he is free from his promise, if only…"

After a long pause, Wesley said, "Yes? If only what?"

"If only he will repay me the one-thousand dollars he borrowed from me."

♦ ♦ ♦

Wesley was walking back toward Phillip's house when he found his way blocked by a horse. He stopped and looked up and saw his brother Skylar sitting in the saddle. "Skylar," he said, too loudly, "you frightened me."

"I saw you coming out of Katherine's house," Skylar said. "I was looking for you anyway. I wanted to have a talk with you."

"I was just walking back to Father's house," said Wesley.

Skylar dismounted to walk alongside Wesley, leading his horse. "Yes," he said, "of course. Well, anyway, it's not his house. It's mine. He's trying to steal it from me along with all my money. But I guess you knew that."

"No. I don't know any such thing."

"Well, it's true. The house belonged to my mother. When she died, he just kept all the papers. She left me a deal of money too, and he's kept that from me. It all belongs to me. Everything he has, and I mean to get it from him, too, one way or another."

"I hope you won't do anything rash," said Wesley.

"You shouldn't worry about what I might do," Skylar said. "But more to the point, what were you doing at Katherine's house, if I may ask?"

"Of course you may ask. She sent for me. She sent a note by the Stinker. Here it is." He pulled the note out of his pocket and handed it to Skylar, who read it and handed it back.

"It doesn't tell much," Skylar said. "What did she want?"

"She wanted to know if you truly want to break your engagement."

"And you told her?"

"I told her that I believe you do."

"Good. And then?"

"She said that you could be free when..."

"When?"

"When you have repaid her thousand dollars."

"Damn," said Skylar. "I was afraid of that. I did take money from her, like a cad. And I will repay it, some way. If only the old fart our father would give me my money all my problems would be solved."

"Can you prove that it's your money?"

"I don't know. He has kept the papers. I could kill him and steal the papers, although I don't think it could be called stealing."

"No, but it could be called murder."

"It should be called only ridding the countryside of a wild animal."

"Skylar, he is your father."

"That hardly matters, Wesley. My mother was a Cherokee, and according to the ways of her people, my people, I was born into her clan. I'm a Wolf person. Perhaps that's why I'm so wild. Anyway, the father is practically irrelevant. He belongs to a different clan, or as

47

in the case of our father to no clan at all, since he's a white man. Gray Mouse is more important in my life than is our father."

"Does Gray Mouse know about the papers?"

"I don't know," said Skylar. "Wesley, I'm glad you have come back. I can talk to you, and you listen. There's no one else I can talk to. Just you. You are like a brother to me, even though we have different mothers."

"We have the same father, and so we are brothers."

"Perhaps there's enough white man in me that I should accept that."

"Skylar," said Wesley, looking deep into the eyes of his brother, "if not for your own sake, then for mine, don't think of becoming a patricide."

When Wesley returned to Phillip Garret's house, he found Phillip sitting at the table with Keenan drinking brandy. Phillip greeted him gregariously and poured him a glass of brandy. Wesley thought of protesting, but he did not. Instead, he sat down and lifted the glass. The thoughts returned to his head about all men being alike, about having a wild and brutal streak running through their bodies. He tipped the glass back and drank. He very nearly drained the glass at one draught.

"Ah," said Phillip, "that's drinking like a Garret. Here. Let me refill your glass." He poured the glass full again and then refilled his own and Keenan's. "Now tell me, my boy, where have you been all this while? In a lady's bed?"

"I have been visiting with a lady. Sitting up in her parlor sipping coffee, and then I had a long visit with my brother, Skylar."

"Skylar?" said Keenan.

"That dog," said Phillip.

"That dog is your son," said Wesley.

"I know that the lady sent you a note," said Phillip, "but how came you to visit with Skylar?"

"I ran into him on the street," said Wesley.

"And what did you talk about?"

"He asked me what the lady and I visited about."

"And you told him?"

"I told him that the lady would release him from their engagement when he repaid her the thousand dollars he owes her."

"So the scoundrel has borrowed money from a woman," said Phillip.

"I'm afraid so," said Wesley.

"That's shameful," said Keenan. "But I'm afraid that he won't let that stop him."

"What do you mean?" asked Wesley.

"He will just go on behaving as if he had never been engaged. That's all."

Wesley turned to his father. "Skylar says that you owe him money," he said. "In fact, he says that he owns this house."

"Nonsense," roared Phillip. "He owes me money. For years I sent him money regularly. I decided I had sent him enough. He'll never pay me back."

Wesley wondered whom he should believe. He believed that his father was capable of telling a lie for any reason, and certainly for a profit. He was not sure of Skylar. Skylar was for sure a womanizer, a gambler and a drinker. He could easily be a liar as well. He was also a threatened parricide. Wesley had heard him now on two different occasions make such a threat. He tipped back his glass and emptied it.

He was beginning to feel a little light headed.

When Wesley and Skylar had parted, Skylar had headed to a different part of the city, a part where the homes were much smaller and more dilapidated. Where doors hung on one hinge, and lawns were ragged. Where horses and goats grazed in front yards and nearly naked children ran freely in the streets. And where white folks might have Indian or Black neighbors on either side. Where sounds of domestic quarrels could clearly be heard from outside. Skylar rode up to a house that was neat enough for the neighborhood. He stopped near the porch and tied his horse to a post that was holding up the roof over the porch. He walked up to the front door and knocked.

The door was opened by a tall man in an expensive dress suit. "Is Adaline at home?" Skylar asked. "Of course," the man said. Skylar pushed his way past the man. There were two other men in the room and two women. Adaline was sitting on the couch with a drink in her hand. The others all had drinks as well.

"Skylar," said Adaline. "Come in and pour yourself a drink."

Instead he walked over to the couch and said to Adaline, "Clear these people out of the house."

"Why should I?"

"So we can talk."

"Get a drink. Sit down here beside me. We can talk."

"I can't talk to you with all these strangers here."

"Nonsense," she said.

"Damn it," shouted Skylar, turning to face the room in general and pulling two Colts out from under his coat. "Get out. Get out of here. All of you."

"What's the meaning of this?" said the man who had opened the door.

Skylar fired a shot over the man's head, and the room was suddenly cleared except for Skylar and Adaline. Adaline jumped up from the couch and moved directly in front of Skylar. She looked him hard in the eyes. "What do you think you're doing?" she demanded.

"I just invited your guests out," he said.

"Are you trying to take over my house?" she said. "This is my house."

"And I love you," said Skylar. He put his guns away. "I love you with all my heart. I want you to be my wife. I don't want these fools hanging around you."

"You're lucky one of them wasn't your own father."

"That old fool," snapped Skylar. "I'd kill him sooner than the others."

"Your own father?"

"Him above all."

"Skylar, if you're not careful, you'll wind up at the end of a rope."

He dropped to his knees and put his arms around her legs. Looking up into her face, with tears suddenly streaming down his face, he cried, "I would hang a dozen times for love of you."

Adaline got down to her own knees facing him, and she embraced him. They kissed passionately and rolled over on their sides on the floor. Skylar's hands roved to her breasts as he moved on top of her. "Adaline," he said. "I love you."

"Oh, Skylar," she moaned.

Just a Man

◆ ◆ ◆

Wesley made his way back to the mission. As he rode his old mare up toward the front door, he noticed several Cherokee boys moping around the front porch. He dismounted, and one of them ran over to tie his horse for him. "My boy," said Wesley.

"Yes sir?" said the boy, a lad of about eleven years old.

"Why is everyone so morose?"

"It's Reverend Wright, sir," the boy said. "He's very sick. They say he is about to die."

Ah, no, thought Wesley. Why did he send me away at such a time? About to die? It mustn't be. I need him yet.

"Thank you," he said to the boy, and then he hurried up to the door and rushed into the building. The boys' teacher, Mr. Drum, met him as he went in. "Is Reverend Wright in his bed?" Wesley asked.

"Yes, he is," Drum answered. "I'm afraid he's very ill. I'm afraid he's…"

"Not long for this world? Yes. I've heard," Wesley said, and he hurried on past the teacher and toward the room which was occupied by the reverend. It took all of his will power to keep from bursting through the door, but he paused just outside the room, and rapped lightly. A small, weak voice came to him from the other side of the door.

"Come in," it said.

Wesley opened the door and stepped inside, slowly, quietly, politely. He shut the door behind himself and looked over toward the bed. Reverend Wright seemed light as a dried leaf. He looked very old and very small and weak indeed. A smile spread across his drawn old face when he saw Wesley.

"Ah, Wesley, so you have come to visit me at last. It's good to see you, my son."

"You speak as if I had been negligent, Reverend," said Wesley, his voice a bit defensive. "You have no right to speak to me like that. It was you who sent me away. Why did you send me away when you were so ill? I should have stayed with you, at a time like this."

"No, Wesley. Your place, as I told you, is with your father and your brothers. Your family is at each other's throats just now, and that is not good. You are a calming agent, and you must be there. Had I died before you came back to visit me, it would not have been a great misfortune. I knew that your thoughts were with me. I know that you love me, and you know that I love you. I would have passed on to the other world easily and smoothly. Even so, I am glad to see you one more time."

"One..."

"Yes. This last time, Wesley."

"Reverend, don't say that. Please."

"Now, now, we must face the facts. I'm dying. I know it, and you must know it. You must accept it. You can live your life and do what you must do without me."

"But I lack your strength, Reverend."

"Rely on the Lord."

"I need your wisdom to guide me."

"God guideth whom he will."

"That is from the Koran, isn't it?"

"Yes. 'But where shall wisdom be found? And where is the place of understanding?' And that is from Job."

"I recognize Job, of course."

"You have all the knowledge and all the guidance you'll ever need."

Tears welled up in Wesley's eyes, and he fought to keep them in there. He did not want the reverend to see them running down his face. It was not that he was afraid of appearing unmanly. It was—he did not know. It was something else altogether.

"My son," said the old man, "be comforted. I go to a better rest than I have ever known. And you go to better things than you have ever known. I'm sorry, but I must sleep now."

"Forgive me for troubling you at this time, Reverend."

"There is nothing to forgive."

"I'll be just outside if you should want me for anything."

Wesley went back to the main room where Drum approached him with an inquisitive look on his pudgy face. "He's resting now," Wesley said.

"May I get you a cup of coffee?" said Drum.

"Thank you." Wesley sat down at one of the dining tables, and Drum brought him a cup of coffee, steaming hot. He had a second cup for himself.

"May I join you?" he asked.

"Of course," said Wesley.

"Have you known Reverend Wright for a long while?"

"I met him while I was in college. He came to preach to us, and I was taken with his intellect and with his forthrightness. I believed then, and I still believe, that I never met a man more brilliant and more honest. I made it a point to meet him, and I flatter myself that we became good friends. I learned that he was coming here to this mission. My home is here in Fort Smith, so I left school and returned home in order to be near him."

"Was it worth it to you. I mean, leaving school and all?"

"Yes, of course. I learn more from Reverend Wright in a brief conversation than I could ever learn from the pedantic professors in a school term."

"So, would you call him your mentor?"

"Mentor, friend, father, all of that and more."

"You sound like you almost worship him."

"'With what deep worship I have still adored the spirit of divinest Liberty.'"

"He is a man," said Drum.

"'I shall not look upon his like again.'"

"I suppose not," said Drum. He finished off his coffee, got up and left.

It was perhaps an hour later when someone came out of the reverend's room to announce that he was dead.

Wesley was stunned. He stood up slowly and trudged heavily to the reverend's room. He went inside and walked over to stand beside the bed, staring down at what had been his mentor, friend and surrogate father. He astonished himself by noticing how insignificant the remains appeared to be.

He wondered at the life and vivacity that had existed in that tiny shell just an hour or so before. He marveled at the way in which he had groveled before this man when he lived. He dropped to his knees, took the dead man's hand in both of his, and wept.

Wesley at last got up and went outside. He mounted his horse and rode slowly back to his father's house. He was not surprised to find his brother Keenan and his father, Phillip, both still seated at the table, both drinking brandy. It was their usual habit these days.

"Wesley," said Keenan, "you look glum."

Wesley took a chair at the table and sat down. "Reverend Wright has died," he said. "He is no more."

"'He lives in fame that died in virtue's cause,'" Keenan said.

"'For he being dead, with him is beauty slain, And, beauty dead, black chaos comes again,'" said Wesley.

"What is this?" shouted Phillip. "Both of you spouting Shakespeare? Or is it something else?"

"You are right, Father," said Keenan. "I spouted from *Titus Andronicus*, and Wesley responded by spewing forth some lines from *Venus and Adonis*."

"What has the death of this preacher to do with Shakespeare?"

"In my brother's eyes," said Keenan, "this man was a great man, a very worthy man, Father, and we were both challenged to quote some words from the greatest of all writers at his passing."

"Humph," snorted Phillip. "I would think a few appropriate words from the Good Book would be more to the point."

"What do you know of the Good Book?" Keenan said.

"Ashes to ashes," said Phillip.

"You of all people."

"Dust to dust."

"Father," said Wesley, "don't blaspheme."

"He died in a good old age, full of days, riches and honor," said Keenan.

"That was appropriate," said Wesley. "Thank you for that one."

"I remember one now," said Phillip gleefully. "'There is death in the pot.'"

"'Who is this that darkeneth counsel by words without knowledge?'" said Keenan. "I think that's enough of that."

"How can you say that?" said Phillip. "Your brother is in need of comforting words."

"I'm all right," said Wesley.

"You see," said Keenan. "He's all right."

"All right then, we'll change the subject to something more cheerful. Your other brother stopped by to see me today..."

"Out of filial devotion, I assume," said Keenan.

"You mean Skylar?" said Wesley.

"Who else would I mean?" said Phillip.

Wesley, of course, was thinking of the Stinker, but he chose to hold his tongue. "What did he want?" he asked.

"He wanted money, of course," said Phillip. "He has never contacted me for any other reason. He claimed to own this very house. The dreamer. The fool."

"He told me this house was his mother's," said Wesley, "and she left it to him."

"Bah. He's a dreamer and a fool, and a fool and his money are soon parted. He wanted money to help him court Adaline. Of all the nerve. He wanted me to give him money with which to court the woman who will be my next wife."

"He tells me that she will be his wife," said Wesley.

"Damn him," shouted Phillip. "He's a liar and a scoundrel. You believe him? How could you believe him, a liar and a scoundrel?"

"And you, Father?" said Keenan. "Are you not a liar and a scoundrel? I've heard you say as much a dozen times."

Phillip suddenly roared with laughter. "You're right, of course, so Skylar is just a chip off the old block, isn't he? But there is nothing the old block hates more than a chip that has come off it. And I say, damn him all the way to hell."

Wesley suddenly felt like he could take no more. He excused himself and went up to bed, but when he stepped into the room with a lighted candle, he saw a bottle of brandy and a glass sitting on the table in the room. "So," he said to himself, "the Stinker has been here."

He thought about Reverend Wright. He thought about Drum, and he thought about his father and Keenan. Finally he thought about Skylar. He wondered once again about all men being scoundrels underneath it all. Am I base and vile? he asked himself. He picked up the brandy bottle by the neck and held it up to the candle, allowing the light to play through the glass and the colored liquid inside. He stared at it for a moment. Then he set the candle on the table and uncorked the bottle. He poured himself a drink.

He sat down in the chair and tilted back the glass, taking a healthy swallow. He was beginning to like the taste of brandy. He thought about some lines he had read from that English poet who had become so popular, even in America, Lord Byron. "Man, being reasonable, must get drunk. The best of life is but intoxication."

Wesley did not sleep well that night. He spent the whole time tossing in his bed, fighting off horrible and ghastly images of naked and partially disrobed women in suggestive postures, images of his father and his brothers in poses with women, and even himself naked and crawling around among several such lewd females.

When Wesley awoke in the morning, he dressed hurriedly and went downstairs to the dining table. The Stinker was there with freshly brewed coffee, cooked bacon and nearly done potatoes and eggs. When he sat down, the Stinker poured him some coffee. Keenan came in almost immediately after Wesley. The Stinker poured him some coffee. Phillip's brandy was still sitting on the table from the night before. Even before he knew what he was doing, Wesley reached for the brandy and poured some into his cup.

"Do you see what is happening to me because of my association with you?" he said.

"What?" said Keenan. "Your association with me? What are you talking about, Brother?"

"I am just out of bed first thing in the morning, and I am pouring brandy into my coffee," said Wesley. "I never did that before. And it's not just you, Keenan. It's you and Skylar and Father. You're all corrupting influences."

"What about me, Brother?" said the Stinker. "Am I not equally corrupting? I too am a Garret."

"Yes," said Wesley. "Yes. You, too. I found the brandy you left in my room. And I drank from the bottle last night before going to bed."

"And did that hurt you, Wesley?" Keenan asked. "And did any of us hold a gun to your head and make you drink the stuff?"

"No. No, you did not. Most likely, I was base and corrupt when I was born. The vileness was hidden deep inside and is just now coming out, perhaps as a result of your influence. Perhaps it would have come out of its own. Oh, I am vile."

"You're not vile, Wesley," said Keenan.

"No," said Wesley, somewhat calmed. "No, I am probably just a man."

"Ha," laughed the Stinker, "and that explains everything. Eat up, brothers, and let's go outside and fuck some pigs. Father just bought some new ones."

Just then Phillip came stumbling in. "Whose father, you damned nigger bastard?" he roared. "I hope you weren't speaking of me. No one ever gave you permission to speak of me in that manner, God damn you straight to hell."

Is it just because I'm a man? Wesley asked himself. *Or is it because I'm a Garret? I have to fight this thing that I've discovered in myself.* And then he reached for the cup and took a great gulp. It tasted good to him.

"Well," said Phillip, "if you boys really want to go out back and fuck my new sows, go right ahead and help yourselves. And when you've satisfied yourselves on them, kill one and roast her. She should taste better for having been satisfied."

Wesley got up abruptly and excused himself, thinking that he could bear no more of this, the crudeness of his own family. He excused himself and left the room hurriedly. Phillip roared with laughter.

"He can't take it, can he? Ha ha. He's been spoiled by the company of preachers. Goddamned God-talking preachers. They've ruined my sweet son, my baby boy. Ha ha. We'll soon cure him of that, if he stays around here long enough. Isn't it ironic that the old preacher sent him away and to us? If only he had known what he was doing."

"Perhaps he did know, Father," said Keenan. "Perhaps he was thinking that Wesley might influence us to more Godly behavior rather than the other way around."

"Perhaps you're right, my boy. But if that is the case, the more fool the preacher."

The Horse Thief

♦ ♦ ♦

Reverend Wright's funeral was scheduled for the next day, and Wesley meant to be there. He was up and dressed early and out of the house. He did not want to be infected by his father or either of his two brothers who were living in the house. Jacob saw him headed for the barn and hurried to meet him.

"You going somewhere, Mr. Wesley? Can I saddle your horse for you?"

"Thank you, Jacob. Yes. I'm going to the mission for the funeral of Reverend Wright."

"Oh, yes, sir. That was a great man, sir."

"Yes, he was, indeed."

Jacob hurried to saddle the horse, and Wesley mounted up and started riding toward the mission. When he had gotten into the town, he heard a commotion. He stopped his horse and looked around to see a gang of boys, white boys, chasing another boy, an Indian. He rode after them and caught up with them just as they caught the Indian boy. They all jumped on the lone boy and began pounding on him. Wesley dismounted quickly and began grabbing the boys one at a time and flinging them away until the Indian boy was free.

"Here. Here," he said. "What is all this? What are you doing?"

"He just deserves a good thrashing," said one of the white boys.

"I suppose we all deserve a good thrashing," said Wesley, "but that doesn't mean that you are appointed to do the job. So many of you against one. That's cowardly. Besides, you might have killed him."

"And I might kill them," said the Indian boy. "One at a time, with a gun."

"Here now," said Wesley. "That's no way to talk."

"I'll do it anyway."

"You just try it," said one of the white boys.

"I know where you all live," said the Indian boy. "I'll wait for you each outside your home, and when you come or go, I'll shoot you dead."

"All right," said Wesley, "all of you boys get on home now, or were you on your way to school?"

"To school," said the white boys.

"All right. On with you then."

While Wesley was occupied with the white boys, the Indian boy jumped into his saddle and kicked the horse in the sides. Wesley heard and turned just in time to see him racing away.

"Hey, you," he shouted. "Come back with my horse."

Some of the white boys laughed. One of them stepped forward to speak to Wesley. "You see?" he said. "He's a thief. He's a no good thieving redskin. You ought to have let us thrash him good. So what if we had killed him? He's no good."

"That's not a Christian attitude," said Wesley. "We're all God's children. That boy, too. And we should treat one another as such. Be kind to others, and you will be rewarded."

"I've heard that before," said the white boy. "I don't think it means Indians though. He stole your horse."

"It means all people, all human beings, equally. He's a child of God."

"Not him."

"Do you know his name?" Wesley asked.

"Charley," said the boy.

"Charley Fox," said another.

"Come on. We'll be late."

The boys all turned and ran away, leaving Wesley alone and on foot. He considered walking to the sheriff's office to report the theft of his horse, but right away he rejected that notion. He started walking toward the mission. He had time.

As he walked along, he thought about the boys. They were so young, and already they were mean and base. They learned it, of course, from their parents. Or did they? Perhaps it was in them when they were born. He had not seen much of infants, but he had seen a few. He knew that they were totally selfish. They screamed and cried when they wanted something. They laughed and cooed when they were satisfied. Where was the difference with adults? He could not tell.

People said that the Indians were uncivilized. They were like babes. The white man had to civilize them, teach them to behave properly. And what was civilization? Wesley thought that it must only be learning to think of others as well as one's self. To be unselfish, to be considerate of others.

What was the use? That sort of teaching only worked in a few cases, on people like Reverend Wright, and then they grew old and died before they were able to influence enough other people.

His legs began to tire, and he was breathing heavily by the time he reached the mission. The coffin was on display in the main room of the mission's dining hall. The people were gathering to listen to the preacher say some words over the body. A table of food was prepared. Wesley found himself a seat. Almost as soon as he was seated, the preacher stepped up behind the podium and asked everyone to stand.

Wesley waited for words of great wisdom, but none came. The words were the same as might have been said over any dead body. Wesley was greatly disappointed. He was angered. He wanted to berate the man for his lack of sensitivity, of decorum, for his failure to recognize the greatness of the man he was sermonizing over. When the preaching was over the congregation paraded by the coffin.

Wesley went with them. He was one of them. When he came to the coffin, he stopped and stared at the remains of Reverend Wright. Was this all? Was this the sum of the man's life? This withered shell?

Was this what it all came down to? He realized that he was holding up the line, and so he moved on.

He did not follow when the crowd went out to the cemetery with the coffin to put it in the ground and cover it over with dirt. He sat alone in the hall and wondered if all feeling was indeed gone from that form. Would it wail underneath the ground? Would it try to scratch its way out of the coffin?

Would it be afraid to be alone in the deep darkness of the grave? Would it worry that it had not finished the work it had been put on earth to accomplish?

He realized that he was weeping silently when the people came back inside. They all rushed to the table of food. Wesley was hungry, but he could not at first bring himself to rush to the table. It did not seem quite proper. Finally he told himself that it would be like his last meal with Reverend Wright, so he got up and walked to the table and got himself a modest meal. He found a seat off to himself to sit and eat, and he thought about the reverend the whole time. He wondered if it would be all right for him to talk to the reverend, or if that would be like he was setting up the reverend as a God. Would it be like praying? He did not know the answer to that, and he did not know anyone who could answer it for him other than the dead man. He thought about the school boys again, and he wondered what Reverend Wright would have said to them. Would the reverend have reported Charley Fox as a horse thief?

Charley rode hard and fast on Wesley's horse. He rode out of town and across the prairie. Soon he found himself riding beside the woods that grew alongside the river. He was wondering where he should go. He knew that he could not return to school. And the school was his only home. He was an orphan, alone in the world, and the school had taken him in. It gave him a place to sleep and food to eat. But he did not need it badly enough to put up the things he had to put up with. The taunting from white boys in town, the teaching that told him his father and grandfathers were all wrong, were all misguided fools who would wind up in hell, the infernal preaching that he pretended to believe but did not really.

He had heard that indigent people lived along the river. No one bothered them there. He decided that he could stay there, at least for a time. The river bank was only a few feet. Then it ran into a steep ledge. Charley rode down to the narrow bank and rode along until he spotted a small cave in the side of the ledge. He dismounted and poked his head into the cave. It was not very deep, but he thought it would be sufficient. Then he wondered about the horse. Anyone riding by would see it there and might investigate. He thought about turning it loose, but he really did need it to get around. He stood there looking around, and he saw the woods. That would be a good place to hide the horse. The woods were thick.

The Killer

♦ ♦ ♦

Wesley stayed at the mission that night, resting, grieving, praying and talking to the spirit of Reverend Wright. The teachers and the rest of the mission staff left him pretty much to himself, although they did notify him when breakfast was ready, and he did eat with them. Then he walked back to his father's house. On the way, he kept alert for any sign of his horse or of the Indian boy, Charley Fox, but he saw no sign of either. When he at last arrived at the house, he was not tired. He noticed Skylar's horse tied at the rail in front of the house.

He went inside and found his father, Keenan and Skylar seated around the table with a bottle of brandy in their midst. The Stinker was waiting on them, although there was little for him to do at this time. They had already had their breakfast. Skylar jumped up quickly and grabbed Wesley's hand to pump it.

"Wesley," he said, "how good to see you, Brother. I've been away to my home in Webber's Falls in the Cherokee Nation for too long. I was hoping to see you. I'm delighted. Sit down."

"I'm afraid I shall not be very good company," Wesley said. "I've just returned from the mission. They buried Reverend Wright today."

"'Let no one pay me honor with tears, nor celebrate my funeral rites with weeping,'" said Keenan. "Quintus Ennius, if anyone is interested."

"Well, no one is, damn you," said Phillip. "What's a Quinis Anus? Not Shakespeare or the Bible. Come, Wesley, sit down. Sit down and have a bit of brandy. It'll do you good after such an ordeal."

Wesley sat down in a chair next to Skylar. "Perhaps you're right, Father," he said. "Perhaps it will do me good." Stinker quickly fetched a glass and poured it full of brandy. He put the glass down on the table in front of Wesley. "Thank you," Wesley said. "I insist that my brother Stinker sit with us with his own glass."

"What?" said Phillip.

"Of course," said Skylar. "Why not? He's a Garret, I've heard. A bastard and a nigger, but a Garret nonetheless."

Stinker sat down.

"Then we shall need Jacob here to serve us," said Phillip. "Jacob. Oh, Jacob!"

"We don't need Jacob," said Wesley. "We can each of us pour from a bottle." He lifted his glass and took a sip. "Actually, I have an intellectual question for Keenan."

"For me? Well, let's hear it at once."

"I know you are an atheist, Keenan," said Wesley, "but I also know that you have written articles on theology and have argued Biblical points with clergy on occasion."

"That's true enough," said Keenan.

"I want to know what you think about a certain matter."

"Let's hear it."

"If a man talks to the spirit of a dead man, is it all right? Or does it mean that he is praying and putting the dead up as a God? Is it blasphemous?"

"I should say it depends on what the supplicant is thinking in his own mind," said Keenan. "Is he praying to that deceased for something that he wants? Is he thanking him for the things around him? Then he is praying, and he is violating the commandment, 'Thou shalt have no other gods before me.' But if he is just communicating as he did with the man when he was alive, then I should see no problem."

"But if he ask for guidance—

"Then I should say he is praying."

"And will he go to hell then?" said Phillip gleefully.

"That is not an intellectual question," said Keenan. "It's theological, and I, as Wesley has pointed out, am an atheist."

Skylar, tired of being left out of the conversation and having no interest in the topic, decided to change the subject. "Did you hear about the dead boy in town?" he asked.

"What dead boy?" said Phillip.

"I've forgotten his name," said Skylar. "He was found in the street in front of his house. A schoolboy."

"Was it some sort of accident?" asked Keenan.

"Murder," said Skylar. "The lad was shot five times in the chest."

"Killed?" asked Phillip.

71

"Deader than a salted slug," said Skylar.

"A white boy?" said Wesley.

"Yes."

"There will be more," said Wesley almost under his breath.

"What's that you say?" said Phillip.

"Nothing."

"Oh, yes, it was," said Skylar. "You said, 'there will be more.' What made you say that?"

"Come on, Wesley," said Phillip. "Tell us."

"What do you know, brother?" said Keenan. "It's obvious you know something. Tell us."

Wesley took another swig of his brandy. He thought for a moment. Then he said, "I was riding to the mission yesterday, when I came across, I think it was six boys, chasing another boy. They caught him and started beating him. I stopped, dismounted and separated them. The six were white boys, and the lad they were beating was an Indian."

"A Cherokee?" said Skylar.

"I couldn't be sure," said Wesley. "I remonstrated with them regarding their cowardice and lack of Christian virtues. The Indian boy said that he would get a gun and kill them one at a time. He said he knew where they each lived."

"By God," said Phillip. "He's the one."

"The other boys began saying that he deserved no better, because he was a lying, thieving redskin. I was talking with them some more when the Indian boy jumped on my horse and escaped."

"So they were right about him, of course. He proved what they were saying. Wesley, you must go at once to the sheriff and report all this."

"No," said Skylar. "He must not. It's not his affair to mess in. Leave it alone, Wesley."

"But he has evidence in a murder case," said Phillip.

"But if this Indian boy is guilty of this murder," said Keenan, "is it not possible that in their savagery the boy's family will seek revenge on the one who identifies him as the culprit?"

"Why are you all so anxious to believe this boy is guilty?" said Skylar.

"Because he's a savage Indian," said Phillip.

"And because he threatened to kill them," said Keenan. "It's too much coincidence."

"I don't even know the boy's name," said Wesley, lying.

"But he has your horse," said Phillip. "That in itself is enough to hang him."

"These Cherokee children know nothing but war," said Skylar. "Violence. After the Trail of Tears, a civil war broke out among them. They were divided into two camps, and they were killing each other. It lasted into the eighteen-forties. Shortly after that, the American Civil War started, and they divided up again. This time into pro-Northerners and pro-Southerners. You all remember that. Once again Cherokees were killing Cherokees. And that war has been over but a few short years. It's not the boy's fault. He grew up amidst war and killing. If someone beats him, killing is the only recourse he knows."

"But he can learn to overcome that," said Wesley.

"Whose side are you on, Brother?" said Skylar.

"Of justice," said Wesley.

"And justice cries out for a hanging," shouted Phillip.

"He's just a boy," said Wesley.

"And a Cherokee boy at that," said Skylar. "These white men will never change their minds, and neither will I."

"With all of you, it's just an intellectual argument," said Wesley, "a debate. I have to make a decision. Do I protect a murderer, a lone and frightened boy, or do I take sides against him with the law and the bullies who beat him and threatened him?"

"What makes you think the little shit is frightened?" said Phillip. "These savages don't frighten easily. They will fight a bear empty handed. They have no feelings."

Skylar stood up. "We have feelings, Father, as much as you or any other white man has." He picked up his glass and tossed down the rest of his brandy. Then he walked to the front door and left the house. Wesley followed him out.

"Skylar," he called. "Wait. I want to talk to you."

Skylar stopped at the foot of the porch steps. "What is it, Wesley?"

"You believe I should keep quiet about all this?"

"I do."

"But if it is this boy, and by the way, his name is Charley Fox, if it is him, he may attempt to kill the other five boys."

"Let the events unfold as they will, Brother. Let them unfold."

Charley Fox

♦ ♦ ♦

Wesley was greatly troubled by his brother Skylar's assessment of the situation. Just let the events unfold. In other words, let the boy continue his murders. It seemed like an unconscionable reaction to the problem Wesley was facing. There were five more boys waiting in line to be killed. Mere boys! Not to mention the damage that would be done to Charley Fox's soul, to become a mass murderer at such a young age.

But what were the alternatives? To turn the lad in to the authorities? That seemed as bad to Wesley as the other way. The boy had been hounded, teased, insulted by the white boys. He was only defending himself. Nothing more. Defending himself in the only way he knew how. As Skylar had said, the only way Charley knew, had known all his life, was violence. And the white boys had said that they would kill him, beat him to death. They said that it was all he deserved, being a red-skinned thief. If he killed them, would it not be self-defense?

He wondered what words of wisdom Reverend Wright might have had for him, had he still been alive. He wished the old man had not died, not just yet at least. What would the reverend have done had it been he who had witnessed those terrible events? Finally, what had he, Wesley, done to deserve being the only witness and the only one to have such a dreadful decision to make?

He considered his options. He could put the whole thing out of his mind. Let the events unfold, as Skylar had said. What would happen would happen, and Wesley would have nothing to do with it.

But he would have. As the five other white boys were killed, he would have made himself an accomplice to their murders. That was unthinkable. He could go to the law and tell them what he had seen, report his stolen horse, tell about the threats, and let the law worry about what to do. But suppose they should hang the boy. What then? Wesley would have been an accomplice to the hanging of a child. That too was unthinkable.

Did he have yet other options? Of course. He could try to locate the white boys and warn them, warn their parents. Have them be at least on the alert. But would that stop Charley? Possibly not. And the parents would certainly tell the law, and that would be the same as if Wesley had gone to the law in the first place. No. That was no good.

He could try to locate Charley Fox and talk to him. He could talk sense to the boy and reason with him. Surely he was old enough to understand that. He could suggest to Charley and his parents that they should move to the safety and security of the Cherokee Nation for Charley's sake. If Charley would agree to abandon his mad search for revenge on the white boys, Wesley would keep his mouth shut. That seemed like a good enough bargain. He almost decided that would be his course of action.

Almost.

He wanted to talk to Skylar again. He wouldn't have minded talking to Keenan again, but he certainly did not want to talk to his father. He already knew what Phillip would say. He knew the old man's prejudices and hatreds. He knew what his father felt about the Indians. His attitudes toward civilization and regarding morality, right and wrong, meant nothing. Phillip simply had no morals. Even Keenan, the self avowed atheist, had a more perfectly defined sense of morality than did his father.

Wesley asked himself how to begin looking for the Indian boy. Surely he went to school. He could make the rounds of the schools and inquire about him. He decided that he would do that, and if he failed to locate him in that fashion, he would enlist the help of Skylar when next he saw him. He wished that he had possessed the good sense to detain Skylar instead of letting him ride away. He would likely be going back to Webber's Falls, and that was beyond Wesley's reach without his horse.

Charley Fox was hiding in the shallow cave down by the river bank. He knew that the white men would kill him if they found out what he had done and if they could catch him. He had a good horse now, but in a way it was a liability. It could be recognized as a stolen horse. While he lurked in the cave, he kept the horse hidden in the nearby woods. He hoped that no one would come across it while he was away hiding.

Charley did not feel that he had done anything wrong. The white men had stolen all of the Cherokee land back in the East and driven the Cherokees to this Western land. They had driven them into a war with the Osages, and they had caused them to engage in a civil war among themselves.

When those two wars had finally ended, they drew the Cherokees into their own Civil War. With all of that done, they were treating the Cherokees badly individually.

Those six white boys were just a small symbol of what was happening between the whites and the Cherokees. And Charley figured that the reason the teachers tried to make the Cherokees Christian was just so they would not fight back, so they would "turn the other cheek." Well, he would not do that. He would fight back. He was not a Christian, although he let the teachers think that he was.

The Search

♦ ♦ ♦

When Wesley arrived back at the mission, the muscles in his legs were hurting and he was panting for his breath. He had made an extra trip from his father's house that day, but it was because he had learned something new, and he had even more to learn. He thought that the information he was seeking was important. It was important to five white boys and to one Cherokee boy, and it was important to everyone who knew those boys, perhaps to everyone in the world. "Inasmuch as ye have done it to one of the least of these my brethren, ye have done it unto me." It was worth a little time and some sore muscles.

At the mission, Wesley located Mr. Drum. "Why, Mr. Garret," said Drum. "What brings you around again so soon?"

"I am searching for a schoolboy," said Wesley.

Drum chuckled. "We have several around here," he said.

"Yes. Of course. I'm looking for a particular boy. A Cherokee boy, I believe. His name is, I think, Charley Fox."

"Oh, yes, Charley is one of ours, but I don't believe he's here just now. He's been truant today, I'm afraid."

So Wesley had located Charley Fox, sort of. He was a student at the mission, but he was not to be found at the mission. And his name was Charley Fox. So that much Wesley knew.

"Do you have a home address for him?" he asked Drum.

"Right here," said Drum. "The boy was orphaned by the war. This is the only home he knows."

Wesley heaved a large sigh. "Do you mind if I sit down and rest a few moments?" he asked.

"Sit down," said Drum. "May I fetch you a cup of coffee? It's reasonably fresh."

"Thank you, Mr. Drum. That's very kind of you."

Drum brought Wesley a cup of steaming coffee, and then excused himself. He had a class to teach. Wesley considered following Drum and listening to what he had to teach the children, but he decided that he had better mind his own business, whatever that was. Just at this point in his life, he wasn't at all sure what his business was. He longed for the advice of Reverend Wright, but he was afraid that if he talked to the good reverend he might be in danger of damning himself. He thought of what Keenan had said about it...

If Wesley had only known that Skylar had not gone back to Webber's Falls. He had instead gone back to the home of Adaline. This time he had found her alone. She had let him in, and she had poured them each a glass of homemade whiskey which she had purchased from a notorious moonshiner.

Skylar took himself a tentative sip. It was good. He took a larger swallow.

"Adaline, my darling, my love," he said, "I had to see you again. I couldn't just ride back to my hovel in Webber's Falls without seeing you. I want you to be my wife, Adaline. I love you. I adore you with all my heart. I don't think I can live without you."

"Of course you can live without me," Adaline said. "Why do men always say such foolish things. If I should go away, you would just fall over dead? Of course you wouldn't. You would go on living. You would find someone else to love, and you would go on."

"I would not. I would not want to. At the very least, I would be like a man lost, like a wanderer in the wasteland. I would not want to find another woman to love. I want you. I want only you."

"Even if I were to marry you," she said, "you would see some other woman, and while I sat at home waiting for you, you would be making love to her, and when you did come home, you would be drunk, and you would lie to me."

"I would not. Never. I swear to you…"

"As your father swears to me. And you are like him in every way. You are a Garret, and you are a lecherous fool just as he is. A lecher and a drunkard. I can see it in both of you."

81

"Adaline, when I can't have you, I take what I can get, but if I had you for my wife, I would no longer want those things. Please, Adaline. Please, my love."

"I don't think I can believe you any more than I can believe him," she said.

"Then kill me now," Skylar said. "Do it at once, and get it over with." He reached inside his coat and pulled out a Navy Colt, holding it butt forward toward her. She stared at it in unbelief. He reached out with his left hand and cocked the pistol. "Here," he said. "Take it. Take it and pull the trigger. You're killing me slowly anyway. Just do it now all at once."

"You're a fool," she said. "Why would I shoot you? To give the law in Fort Smith a reason to hang a woman? Put your silly gun away. Then go away yourself. I don't want you around me when you're acting like that."

"Very well," said Skylar, easing the hammer back down and putting the gun away underneath his coat. No one would have been more surprised than Skylar had Adaline chosen to take the gun and pull the trigger, but she had not. "I won't behave that way any more then," he continued. "Instead, I shall just get drunk."

He drained his glass and then poured it full again of the stout whiskey from the moonshiner.

"I can't stand it when you compare me to that foul and nasty old man. That lecherous old goat. That damnable, bloated, horrible old man."

Look For the Horse

◆ ◆ ◆

Skylar had worn himself out with trying to make love to Adaline. She just would not listen to him. She refused to hear what he was saying to her. He did not believe for a minute that she had any interest in his father. In fact, he believed that she had for old Phillip Garret only contempt. Yet she continually threw him up to Skylar. Was she just using Phillip to keep Skylar off-balance? God, Skylar wished with all his heart that the old man would just die and save him the trouble of killing the old fart.

Skylar rode easily toward the line where Arkansas met the Cherokee Nation. Webber's Falls was only a short distance over the border. He had no reason to remain in Fort Smith since Adaline was being so incredibly perverse with him. He turned a corner to ride west, and he saw a familiar figure walking west along the side of the street. He picked up a little speed and hurried alongside the man.

Sure enough, it was his brother, Wesley.

"Wesley," he said. "Where are you going?"

Wesley was a little startled. He looked over his shoulder to see Skylar riding along on his big, black horse. "Oh, Skylar," he said. "I'm just walking back to Father's house."

"Climb up behind me," said Skylar, "and I'll give you a ride."

"I don't want to put you out."

"Nonsense. I'm riding that direction anyway. Come on."

He held out a hand toward Wesley, who grabbed hold of it and swung up behind the saddle.

"Thank you," he said.

"What's a brother for? Even a half brother? I'm glad I came across you, Wesley. I have just come from Adaline's house, and she was not in a friendly mood. I think I was needing someone to talk to. I'm glad it was you I came across."

"I, too, was wanting to see you," said Wesley.

"Oh? What about?"

"I've been trying to locate Charley Fox. I know you advised me to let well enough alone, but I feel I must talk with him. I have to try, at least."

"What have you tried?"

"I found out that he is a student at the mission, and that he has been living there. He's an orphan. But he didn't show up there last night. Now I don't know where to look."

"That's a real problem," said Skylar. "If the boy has no home in Arkansas, he could be anywhere. He might be sleeping in an alley somewhere in the city. He could be hiding out in the country around here. If he is really bright, he would be in the Cherokee Nation. He has a good horse now. It would be easy for him to ride over there. He could easily find shelter with some Cherokee family. They are notoriously generous with Cherokee orphans. And he might even have changed his name. It's not unusual to find Cherokees these days with two or three or even more surnames: the Cherokee name of their parents, its English translation, and perhaps the name of a family that has taken them in. That makes it even more difficult for the white lawmen to track them down."

"You make it seem like an almost impossible task," said Wesley.

"It could be," said Skylar. "Why is it so important for you to find this boy?"

"I want to try to stop him from becoming a mass murderer."

"A noble pursuit. But if this boy is serious about killing these remaining five white boys, he would not go far from Fort Smith, now would he?"

"I suppose not."

"An idea comes to me."

"What is it?"

"Sometimes when a man has no home in Fort Smith but wants to hang around, he goes to the river at night and sleeps there."

"Where? On the river?"

"Well, not on the water, of course, but along the banks. There is shelter where the bank is high, and there are even caves."

"What should I do then? Just walk down to the river and start walking along the bank and looking?"

"We could ride there right now," said Skylar. "I'm in no great hurry to get to Webber's."

"But I—

"Don't argue with me. You want to find this boy, don't you? And the sooner the better? Let's go. You know, it occurs to me that he might be easy to find if he is down there."

"Why is that?"

"He has your horse. It will be hard to hide a horse. He would most likely put him in the trees along the riverbank. We'll look for the horse."

Why Does It Matter?

◆ ◆ ◆

Wesley was astonished and well pleased when they came across his horse so quickly and easily, hobbled in a clump of trees near the river. *It had taken almost no time to find the beast,* he thought. *Charley Fox could not be far off.*

"Skylar," he said, "I can never thank you enough. I might never have found him on my own."

"Well, then, get down and put the saddle on him," said Skylar.

Wesley dropped off the back of Skylar's horse and ran over to his own. He thought that the creature was glad to see him, but of course that could just have been his imagination. The saddle and blanket lay on the ground just a few feet away, and Wesley had the horse saddled and ready to go in record time. He unfastened the hobbles and tossed them aside. Then he mounted up. He had a wide smile across his face. He rode over beside where Skylar sat on his black.

"Well," he said, "what now?"

"Now we check the river banks nearby."

They rode slowly along the river looking carefully as they went. After they had gone a ways, Skylar urged his horse down the steep bank to the narrow strip that ran along between the high rise and the water. Wesley followed him. "Up there," said Skylar, and he pointed to a spot along the steep bank that was darker than the rest of the bank. He rode on past it a little, and Wesley came up even with it. He squinted at it.

"It looks like a shallow cave," he said.

"Get down and look inside," said his brother.

Wesley got down and bent over to peer into the dark cave, but he suddenly stepped back. From the back of his horse, Skylar could see a hand holding a gun poke out of the darkness.

"Get away from here," came a voice.

"Young man," said Skylar, "I too have a gun in my hand, and I can kill you faster than you can pull your trigger. Come out of there."

There was a pause. The gun coming out of the cave was lowered, and Charley Fox came crawling out. Wesley bent forward and took the gun from the hand. He was uncomfortable with it. He stepped toward Skylar and handed the weapon to him. Skylar took it and dropped it into his coat pocket.

Charley Fox stood up and held his hands up high.

"Did you come to arrest me?" he asked.

"No," said Wesley.

"But he has a gun on me."

"You pointed yours first," said Skylar.

"Well, what do you want? Your horse? Well, you've got him back. Now leave me alone."

"We can't do that, Charley," said Wesley. "You're still a boy. We can't leave you like this."

"Who cares?"

"My brother cares," said Skylar, tucking his gun away beneath his coat. "He cares about everyone in the world." He felt like he was overburdened with revolvers, and he took Charley's revolver back out of his pocket and gave it back to Wesley, who put it in his own pocket.

"Is this your brother?"

"Yes."

Charley looked at Wesley. "I'm sorry I took your horse," he said, "but I needed to get away."

"Besides," said Skylar, "horse stealing is an honored old Cherokee occupation, Right?"

"Yeah," said Charley, a small smile creeping onto his face, "I guess it is."

"Well, come along, Charley," said Wesley.

"Where are you taking me?"

"I'm taking you to my home, to my father's house."

"What if I don't want to go?"

"You don't have any choice, young man," Skylar said. "You're outnumbered, and we're both bigger than you are."

"Then you're a couple of bullies."

"We only have your welfare in mind," said Wesley. "Now, come on."

Wesley mounted up and reached for Charley's hand, swinging him up behind the saddle. Then Skylar and Wesley rode for Phillip's house. Wesley was surprised that Skylar rode along, for from the river, the Garret house was out of Skylar's way. When they reached the house and were putting their horses in the barn, Wesley said, "Did you decide to stay here tonight?"

"Why not?" said Skylar. "He's my father, too, though I'm ashamed to own up to the fact."

They found Phillip and Keenan seated at the table drinking brandy, and Stinker came out of the kitchen and poured glasses of brandy for Skylar and Wesley. "I guess this one's too young," he said nodding toward Charley.

"Yes," said Wesley. "Can you find him something else?"

"Is this your little murderer?" said Phillip.

"No," said Wesley, a little too quickly perhaps. "This is a young scholar I met at the mission. He's an orphan, so I decided to bring him home for a good meal."

"And the other one?" Phillip asked.

"He's my brother."

"This is your brother, right here," said Phillip, pointing to Keenan.

"And so is this," said Wesley.

"What is the young scholar's name?" said Keenan.

"Oh, I beg your pardon. This is Charley Fox. And Charley, this is my father, Phillip Garret, my brothers, Keenan and Skylar." Just then Stinker came out of the kitchen again, carrying a glass for Charley. "And this," Wesley continued, "is my other brother, Stinker."

Charley looked from Skylar to Stinker to Wesley to Keenan and to Phillip He looked back at Wesley. "You three look like white men," he said, "but those two look Indian."

90

"I'm Cherokee," said Skylar. "No one knows exactly what Stinker is. And you're right about the rest. They are white men."

"But you said you're all brothers, and that one is your father."

"We had three different mothers," said Wesley.

"Our father is a dirty old man," said Skylar.

"Oh," said Charley. "So you're half brothers."

"Yes," said Wesley, "except for me and Keenan. We're full brothers."

"Is there a Mrs. Garret?" Charley asked.

"They're all three dead," said Phillip. "Dead and buried and gone to hell, likely."

"Why do you say that?" Charley asked.

"They must have all been terrible sinners to have married our father," said Keenan.

"If I believed in your Bible," said Charley, "I would say that my parents have gone to heaven."

"Hooray," said Keenan, "you really do have a little scholar here."

"Is that all it takes to make a scholar?" asked Wesley. "To deny the Word of God?"

"It's a good beginning, at least," replied Keenan.

"But I'll bet he's not an atheist like you," said Skylar. "Are you?"

"Do you know what an atheist is, boy?" asked Keenan.

"I know."

"Are you an atheist?" asked Wesley.

"No."

"Do you pray?" Skylar asked.

"Yes. Sometimes."

"To whom do you pray?"

"Unelanuh'."

"The lad is a good Cherokee," Skylar said.

"Praying to those heathen gods is just the same as being an atheist," said Phillip.

"You're showing your ignorance and your prejudice once again," said Skylar.

"Keenan," Phillip shouted. "Back up your old father."

"I'm afraid I agree with him," said Keenan. "Any religion is as good as any other."

"Damn. I've raised a bunch of heathens."

"The problem with that statement, dear Father," said Keenan, "is that you didn't raise a one. We were all raised by Jacob and by schools."

"To our great, good fortune," added Skylar.

"I should turn the lot of you out for being ungrateful whelps."

"Mr. Garret," said Charley, "excuse me, but why does it matter to you what your sons think about religion?"

"Thou Shalt Not Kill."

♦ ♦ ♦

"Your father doesn't like me," Charley said to Wesley later when Wesley had gotten them away from the crowd.

"Father doesn't seem to like anyone," Wesley said. "Don't let it worry you."

"But you brought me to his house. I don't like to be in the home of someone who doesn't like me."

"But my brother Skylar claims that it is his home, and I believe that Skylar does like you,"

Wesley said. "He's Indian, like you."

"Yes. We are both Cherokees. What is Skylar's clan?"

"I believe I've heard him say that it's Wolf."

"Then we are related. I'm Wolf clan."

"That's amazing, Charley. So you and my brother are related. Does that make us related too?"

"I don't think so, Wesley, because the relationship is through our mothers."

"Well, that's too bad. I would like to be your brother."

"Why?" said Charley.

"I like you, Charley. As a Christian, I love you. I don't want to see anything bad happen to you. That's why I want you to give up the idea of killing all those boys who beat you. Killing is bad. The Bible says, 'Thou shalt not kill.' I want you to enjoy the good Christian life and the final reward of heaven. Don't you want that for yourself?"

Charley was silent for a moment before saying, "I'm not a Christian. I don't care about your heaven."

"Charley, God sent his son Jesus Christ to earth to live among us for a time and then to die on the cross for our sins, for all of us, regardless of our race and our skin color. He came down here for all men."

"I don't believe he was thinking about me when he was on the cross. Besides, his preachers and teachers tell us that all our ways are wrong, that our fathers and grandfathers were all wrong. Is my father in hell because he kept to our old ways? I can't believe that. I don't want to believe it. I won't believe it."

"I won't argue with you, but I won't give up on you either."

Skylar came storming out of the house to find Wesley and Charley sitting on a bench in front of the house. He walked over to join them. "Our father is impossible," he said. "He's a crazy old man."

"But he is our father," said Wesley. "'Honor thy father and thy mother.'"

"Honor must be earned," said Skylar, "even from a father. And he has earned none. Not from me."

"Skylar?" said Charley.

"What is it?"

"Wesley tells me it's wrong for me to seek revenge against those white boys. The ones who beat me. What do you say?"

"There are two ways of looking at that," Skylar said. "The Bible way says, 'Do good to those who hate you.' The old Cherokee way says that we should take a life for a life to maintain balance. Choose your way."

"The Bible also says, 'An eye for an eye,'" said Wesley. "It does not say, 'A life for an eye.' Those boys only beat you. You don't have a life to avenge."

"No," said Charley. "I guess I don't have. Maybe I shouldn't have…"

"Stop now," said Wesley, "before it's too late."

"Maybe it's already too late for me," Charley said.

"It's never too late," said Wesley.

"For once I agree with my brother," Skylar said.

"But if the law finds out what I did…"

"Then we'll deal with the law when that happens," said Skylar. "For now, you can quit that school and come with me to Webber's Falls in the Cherokee Nation. They won't likely find you over there."

"I thought you were going to stay here tonight," said Wesley.

"We'll stay here tonight, and we'll go to Webber's Falls in the morning."

Charley looked at Skylar and smiled. "All right," he said. "I'll do what you say."

A Prowler

♦ ♦ ♦

Wesley was greatly relieved to have gotten Charley's promise to stop the killing. He really was fond of the lad and did not want to see him get deeper into trouble than he could dig himself out of. It was also good, he told himself, that Charley was going with Skylar back to the Cherokee Nation. With the boy's attitudes, it was probably the best place for him, and Skylar would make a good companion for him.

Phillip sat up drinking until he passed out. Stinker carried him to his bed and put him in it, taking off his boots for him. Phillip moaned and cursed during the whole process, although he did not regain his consciousness, and Keenan and Wesley went to their rooms. Wesley could not sleep. He imagined that he heard someone roaming around through the house. At last he got out of bed and lighted a lamp which he carried with him as he went out of his room to venture through the mansion looking for the source of the disturbance.

He went into every room he came to, but in every room the sounds seemed to come from a little farther away. He went down the stairs and into Phillip's library. There were empty shelves along all four walls. The only books visible were the Bible and a Complete Shakespeare. He turned to go out of the room when a figure showed up in the doorway. All that Wesley could recognize was a large revolver pointed into the room and directly at him. "Hold it," came a somewhat familiar voice. Wesley stood still. He moved the lamp a little bit, and then he at last recognized the figure in the doorway.

"Keenan," he said. "For God's sake, don't shoot. It's me. Your brother. Wesley."

Keenan lowered the hammer on the revolver carefully and lowered the gun. "Wesley," he said.

"What are you up to in here?"

"I thought I could hear someone moving through the house, and I couldn't sleep. So I decided to investigate. What brought you out?"

"The same thing," said Keenan. The two brothers were speaking to one another in barely more than a whisper. "Who could it be, do you think?"

"I can't think of anyone," said Wesley. "It could be a stranger, a burglar."

"It could be, but I doubt it. It could be Skylar skulking around in the dark."

"But he has Charley with him." Wesley protested.

"It could be Charley sneaking through the house as a favor to Skylar, or just looking for something to steal."

"Don't be foolish, Brother," said Wesley. "It could be anyone. Maybe Stinker had some work to finish up."

"Should we check on Father?" Keenan said.

"Let's do."

They hurried on through the house to Phillip's room. The door was shut. Keenan closed his fist on the door knob and looked at Wesley. Wesley nodded, and Keenan opened the door, slowly. He stepped forward and peeped in. Then he pushed the door farther open and stepped into the room. Wesley followed him. Phillip was up, seated at a small table. A candle burned on the table, and a bottle of brandy stood there. Phillip had a glass in front of him. It was about half full of brandy. He was startled when the two brothers stepped into the room. He jumped to his feet.

"Ahh," he shouted. "What is this? You've come to murder me."

"No, Father," said Wesley.

"It's just Wesley and Keenan," said Keenan. "We've not come to do you harm."

"Then what the hell are you here for this time of night? Answer me that. What?"

"Father," said Wesley, "we heard noises, as if it were someone moving through the house."

"We got up to investigate, and we decided we should check on you."

"To make sure that you're all right."

"That's all."

"Well, I'm all right, as you can see," snarled Phillip. "Now go on back to bed."

"Father," said Wesley, "should you be drinking at this hour?"

"Go to bed."

"Good night, Father," said Wesley, and he turned to leave the room.

"Good night," said Keenan.

"Boys," said Phillip. The brothers stopped and turned to look back at their father. "Thank you," he said, "for thinking of me."

As they moved back toward the stairway, Keenan said, "Let's check on the Stinker. Maybe it was he."

"Yes," said Wesley, "it might have been."

They went out the big front door and made their way to the small cabin which was assigned to the Stinker. Wesley thought it was awful to have his own brother committed to such a hovel. It reminded him of a slave's quarters. Perhaps it had been just that at one time. The two brothers got to the cabin and rapped lightly on the door. There was no answer. "What now?" said Wesley to Keenan. Keenan tried the handle on the door, and the door opened. The brothers looked at one another, and they entered the room.

There was no one there.

Katherine and Keenan

♦ ♦ ♦

It was around mid-morning when Keenan saddled his
horse and mounted it to ride away from the house. He
did not know where he was going, or rather, he knew
where he wanted to go, but he was not at all sure that he
would actually go there. It was maybe a forty minute ride
from Phillip's house, and when he got there, he rode on
past the place, looking over his shoulder, longing to go
up to the door. He rode on until he was out of sight of the
house. He stopped, turned his horse around and rode
back. This time he stopped in front of the house and tied
his horse to the hitch rail. Then he just stood there beside
the horse for a long moment. His hand was on the horse's
neck. He stared at the ground. Then he looked up and
stared for a bit at the door. He looked back down at the
ground. At last he summoned all his courage and
stepped up onto the porch. He walked over to the door
and rapped lightly on it. Perhaps no one inside would
hear such a light tapping. He started counting to himself

and told himself that he would wait only until the count of thirty. If no one had answered the door by then, he would leave. He had reached twenty-five when someone opened the door from the inside.

Keenan was startled by the vision that stood there before him. He was suddenly afraid that he was looking the fool. He stammered. "You must be Miss Durwood," he finally managed to get out.

"I am Katherine Durwood," she said. "May I know who you are?"

"Oh, yes. Excuse me, please. You already know my brothers. My brother Wesley, and, of course, you know Skylar. I am Keenan Garret, and your servant."

Katherine stepped back and to one side. She smiled a very pleasant little smile. "Please come in, Mr. Garret," she said.

Keenan walked into the room and looked around. Katherine indicated a chair, and he sat. "May I offer you some coffee?" she said.

"Thank you," he said. "That would be very nice."

Katherine called for her servant to bring out coffee for two. She sat on one end of the sofa and looked at Keenan. "What brings you here, Mr. Garret?" she asked.

"I, uh, it's embarrassing," he said. "I just, well, I wanted to see you, to meet you. My brothers both know you, and I felt sort of –left out."

"Well, are you disappointed?"

"Oh, no, on the contrary. You are, I think, the most beautiful woman I have ever seen."

"Your brother talked like that to me—once."

"My brother, Skylar, is a damned fool," Keenan said. "How could he—"

"He's found himself a new woman," she said, "and that's all there is to it. From what I've heard of your father, it runs in the family. If you were in Skylar's situation, you would probably be doing the same as he."

"Oh, no, Miss Durwood," he said. "Please don't think that of me. If I was so lucky as to have your promise, nothing could draw my affections away from you. Nothing."

"Nothing? Really?"

"In fact, I would work hard all day long, every day, to make you want to hold on to me. My every action would be calculated to keep your attention on me and me alone."

"You're a darling, Keenan. May I call you Keenan?"

"Of course."

"And you must call me Katherine.

"Dear Katherine."

"You know, of course, Keenan, that the only reason I'm holding Skylar to his promise to me is so that I may get back my loan to him of one thousand dollars. I hope you don't think me greedy, holding that against him."

"Of course not, Katherine," said Keenan. "That is a great deal of money, and I know that Skylar has been trying very hard to come up with it."

"I'm sure that he would like very much to be rid of me."

"As I said before, my brother is a damn fool."

"Keenan, I'm very glad that you came by to see me today. I've been feeling low lately. You know, it's not an easy thing for a woman to realize that the man she is engaged to no longer finds her attractive. She begins to believe that she is not so good looking, perhaps that she is growing old."

"Katherine, never think that, and please do not feel low. You have every right to feel pampered and courted and to have the world laid at your feet. Katherine, oh, if I dared, but no, it is much too soon for me to speak."

"Speak, Keenan," she said. "I have needed someone to speak to me for so long now."

"Katherine, if you were not engaged to be married, if you were a free woman, I would beg for your hand."

She patted the sofa beside where she sat, and Keenan moved over there beside her.

"The only reason to delay," she said, "is to get my one thousand dollars back from Skylar. When that happens, I shall release him from his promise. Then, of course, I too shall have been released, and then you may speak freely to me of your desires."

The Broken Window Pane

♦ ♦ ♦

In the middle of the day, old Phillip Garret set out a fresh bottle of ink and got himself a new quill. He poured himself a glass of brandy and sat down at the table. He took a healthy drink and leaned back in his chair to think over what he would write. He had his best paper laid out on the table. He dipped his quill in the ink, and he began to write, carefully, slowly, meticulously, in his best hand.

> My dearest Adaline,
>
> I must see you soon, tonight, here at my house. Come quickly to me, I beg you.
>
> I know that Skylar, my one-time son, has been pleading with you for your hand, but he cannot get his hands on the money he needs to get himself free from that other woman. I, on the other hand, have plenty of money for you. In fact, I have three thousand dollars in cash on hand, hidden in my bedroom. If you will come to me tonight, as I beg of you, I will give it to you to use in outfitting yourself for our wedding.

Please do not disappoint me. I am dying to see you, to hold you in my arms and kiss your sweet lips. Tonight, my love. I'll be waiting anxiously.

Your always devoted, Phillip

He folded the letter up and sealed it with hot wax. Then he stood up, lurched to the door and swung it open, bashing it against the wall, leaned out into the hallway and shouted with all the power in his lungs.

"Stinker. Come here to me at once. Get your black ass up here right now."

Stinker lingered long enough to make the old man scream at him twice more before he appeared at the bedroom door with an inquisitive look on his face. "What is it, Mr. Phillip?" he asked.

"I want you to deliver this at once," Phillip said, handing the letter to Stinker.

"Who does it go to?" Stinker asked.

"Who do you think, fool? It goes to her. To the lovely Adaline. Now go before I decide to beat you. Hurry to her house. At once. Run. Run. Run."

The Stinker took the letter in his hand and turned to run down the hallway. When he reached the front door, he crashed through it, not bothering to stop and shut it behind him.

He ran at full speed toward the front gate. He knew already how far old Phillip could watch him as he ran from the house. He had studied it from Phillip's bedroom window. When he was safely beyond old Garret's eyesight, he quit running. He slowed to a comfortable walk, and he strolled the rest of the way to Adaline's house.

Wesley sat in his room holding the six-gun he had taken away from Charley Fox. He sat on the edge of his bed and held the gun in both hands. He stroked the barrel, feeling the cold, smooth steel. He cocked the hammer back and spun the cylinder. He turned the cylinder slowly and studied the empty chambers, the places from which the bullets that had claimed the white boy's life had sped on their deadly path. Finally he gripped the handle in his right hand and held the gun as if ready to shoot.

He liked the feel of the gun in his hand, and he was more than a little ashamed of that feeling. He wondered if he should have given the weapon back to Charley or to Skylar to keep safe. He was almost sure that Charley no longer planned to kill the rest of the boys. He could let Charley have his gun back. It wasn't any good in Wesley's hands. Wesley wasn't about to shoot anyone, he thought.

The revolver was still cocked. Wesley pointed it at the window, and before he realized what he was doing, he had squeezed the trigger. The roar of the exploding shell was deafening. His ears started ringing. His nostrils were filled with the stench of burning powder. The window glass was shattered. Wesley was startled. He stood up and walked to his bedroom door. He opened the door and looked out. There was no one around.

"It was an accident," he shouted. "No one was harmed. Only a window pane broken. That's all."

In another couple of minutes, old Jacob came to the door. "Mister Wesley?" he said.

"Yes. Jacob. I'm sorry. I was just looking at this pistol." He held it up for Jacob to see, but the way he held it, he almost had it pointed at Jacob. "I was just looking at it, you know? And it went off. I shot the window. You see. Over there. I broke the window, I'm afraid."

Jacob walked slowly to Wesley and held out his hand. "Mr. Wesley," he said, "you ain't used to handling them things. I think maybe you better let me put that away for you."

Wesley looked at the gun in his hand, and he looked at the palm of Jacob's hand. He placed the gun in the former slave's hand. "I'll be right back and clean up that mess," Jacob said, and he walked out the door with the gun in his hand. Wesley missed having it in his hand.

That worried him. He recalled how he had very quickly developed a taste for his father's brandy. Now he was suddenly enjoying the feel of a revolver in his hand. He considered once again the idea that he had been born basically a bad man, a man with the curse of the Garrets in his blood. He was as mean and bad as his brother Skylar, as evil as his atheist brother Keenan and as ugly as his bastard brother the Stinker. "Is there no hope for humanity?" he asked out loud, but who was he asking?

Adaline read the letter from Phillip Garret, and she laughed out loud. The old fool, she thought, there is no way I would put myself that much in his power. To be alone with him in his house indeed. To hell with that old man. She thought of Skylar, his son. How could a father and son be so different? she asked herself, but then she quickly thought, perhaps they are not so different after all. Skylar is engaged to be married to that Durwood woman, and he owes her money. He pleads with me and begs me in much the same way his father does. He has killed men, too, I know. He's a drinker and a gambler. He must be as bad as his father. He must be. Yet he is not.

Keenan rode all the way to Webber's Falls, and he rode around some asking questions of the people he saw there. Only once did he ask a Cherokee man who apparently had no English. He excused himself as best he could and kept asking. At last it occurred to him that Skylar probably had few, if any, friends in Webber's Falls. It had been a Confederate stronghold during the late war, and Skylar had been an officer in the Union Army. He did not walk around displaying a flag or wearing his uniform, but the people in the town likely knew about his past. At last he met someone who knew his brother. The man gave him directions to Skylar's house. Keenan thanked the man and rode on. With the directions, it did not take Keenan long to find his way.

When he finally found the house, he was not much surprised. It was a small log cabin. The yard around it was neat and clean. It had a small covered porch on the front and a corral to one side. Keenan noticed two horses in the corral. There was a hitch rail in front of the house. Keenan rode up to it, dismounted and tied his horse there. Then he walked up onto the porch and to the front door and rapped on it. The door was opened quickly, and Charley Fox stood there looking up at him.

"Well, Charley," said Keenan. "You surprised me. Is my brother in?"

"Of course," said Charley. "Come on in."

Keenan walked into the room, and Skylar stood up from a chair across the way.

"Hello, Brother," he said. "What brings you to the Cherokee Nation?"

Charley indicated a chair, and Keenan sat down. "My purpose can be taken care of quickly," he said, reaching into an inside coat pocket. When his hand came out, it was clutching a stack of bills. "I know that you've been in want of ready cash. I've brought you the cash you need. There's a thousand dollars here, Skylar. Just what you need to pay your debt."

"Why are you doing this?" said Skylar.

"Brotherly love," said Keenan.

"Why should I believe that?"

"All right. I've met your affianced. She wants her money very badly. I felt compelled to try to help her out. Here. Take the money."

"Where did you get it?"

"What difference does that make?"

"I want to know."

"If you must know, I got it from Father."

"Did you steal it from him?"

"I did not. He made me a loan."

"That doesn't seem likely. The old skinflint won't loan me a dime."

"He likes me better than you," said Keenan, with a grin. He stood up, tossed the money down on a table and walked to the door.

"Are you leaving so soon?" said Skylar.

"I told you my business wouldn't take long," said Keenan, and he walked out the door, shutting it behind him. Skylar walked to the table and picked up the money. He started counting it.

The Disengagement/Engagement Party

◆ ◆ ◆

Katherine Durwood had a big gathering at her house in Fort Smith. She invited all the "best" people of the town. Of course, she invited Keenan Garret and his brother Wesley. Skylar was not invited. The judge of the district court was invited. The commander of the fort and other officers from Fort Gibson in the Cherokee Nation were invited. A few members of the council of the Cherokee Nation were invited. The chiefs of all of the so-called Five Civilized Tribes were invited. She had the best foods catered for the occasion. There was fresh shrimp and lobster, fine cuts of beef and pork, crawdads served in the New Orleans style barbecue, with corn, beans, squash, biscuits and cornbread. In short, something for everyone's taste. She had whiskey and champagne, the whiskey was both legal and illegal. She even had some cold beer.

When the crowd was all gathered, her servant rang a little bell to get everyone's attention. Then Katherine got to the front of the room. She held up her hands for silence. All eyes were on her.

"My dear friends," she said, "I thank you all for coming tonight. This is a very special occasion for me. I have an announcement to make. Part of it is a bit embarrassing for me. The remainder is joyous. To begin with let me say that I know that my ill-fated engagement to Captain Skylar Garret was widely known. So was my trouble which followed it. The captain changed his mind and wanted out, desired to be freed from his promise. I refused him. That, I think, also became the talk of the town."

"Dear lady," said the judge, "there are always idle gossips, and we would all be better off if they would keep their mouths shut."

"Yes, your honor," Katherine said. "Thank you for that. But what I want to announce first of all tonight is that I have set the captain free from his promise. The engagement is officially off."

That announcement was greeted with cheers and light applause. Katherine smiled politely at the crowd, and gave a slight curtsy. Then she went on. "I wish to further announce my engagement to Mr. Keenan Garret." She held out a hand to Keenan, and he stepped up to take it and to stand by her side. He smiled broadly for an instant, then stood with a dignified expression, holding her hand and looking out on the crowd with an expression of exuberant pride on his face.

Immediately people began to throng around the two to shake their hands and offer their congratulations. "But Katherine, my dear," said the judge, "isn't this the other young man's brother?"

"Yes, my dear," she said, "but they are as different as night and day."

"I wish you all the good fortune that may befall a newly married couple."

"Thank you."

The small talk went on and on in this manner, until finally it was all rudely interrupted by the abrupt and uninvited entrance of Skylar. "My friends," he shouted, "I'm late, but I hope you'll forgive me. By some oversight, I was not invited. I'm sure it was an oversight, because the purpose of the party involves me as much as anyone. It's to celebrate freeing me up from an undesired engagement."

Keenan, pushing his way through the crowd and toward his brother, said, "Skylar. You're not welcome here. Turn around and take yourself out at once."

Wesley moved toward his two brothers as rapidly as he could manage it. When he reached them, he got himself in between the other two.

"Keenan," he said, "leave this to me, please." He turned to look directly into Skylar's eyes.

"Skylar, please, go away. You don't want to create a disturbance here. You loved Katherine once. You must have. Why else did you become engaged to marry her? Why would you now want to embarrass her? You've caused her enough misery. I beg you to not bring on more."

"You're right, of course, Wesley. I am a thorough beast to behave in this way. I will leave after I apologize to everyone, but first, I want to speak to her. Will you bring her over here, please."

"Promise to make it brief," said Wesley.

"Yes. Of course."

Wesley went back to Katherine and whispered in her ear. She walked with him to where Skylar waited by the front door. She stood stiffly looking him in the face. Skylar bowed.

"Katherine," he said, "I've done you yet another hurt. I apologize deeply. I don't know what came over me to show up here and act the fool in front of you and your guests. The only thing I can think of is the thought that you left me for my own brother, but even that is no excuse. He is a much better choice for you than was I, and I wish you and him much happiness. Forgive me."

He bowed again, and then looking over the still stunned crowd, said, "My friends, I hope you will forgive the effrontery of an old fool." Then he turned and walked out of the house.

The party continued after a few moments of subdued near silence. A few guests got themselves slightly drunk. They all ate their fill, a few more than that. They talked, and then a few got out their instruments, a guitar, a banjo and a violin, and began to play, and then there was dancing. It was getting late when the second unpleasant surprise appeared in the shape of Phillip Garret. He stepped in the door and stood there quietly looking about. When one would spy him and recognize him, that one would be silent and stand still. Soon the whole room was quiet and staring at Phillip.

"What?" said Phillip. "Did I spoil the party? How could I spoil the party? I am only the father of one man who became disengaged and another who became engaged here tonight. And both to the same woman. That merits space in the newspaper. Is there a journalist here? What? No journalist invited? I shall write the story myself and deliver it to the paper in the morning. It will be a great story. You'll all enjoy reading it."

"Father," said Keenan.

"Why wasn't I invited?" roared Phillip.

"Dear Mr. Garret," said Katherine, walking up to him and offering her hand, "it was a ghastly oversight, and I beg your forgiveness for it. It was entirely my fault."

"What a grand lady," said old Garret, "to take the blame completely on herself. But I doubt, daughter, may I call you daughter? I doubt, daughter, the truth of that confession. I believe that my son Keenan, my loving son, was more to blame. I believe that he is ashamed of me and did not want your fine friends here to see me in my dirty and rumpled clothes and did not want to risk having me say something that would embarrass you in front of these people."

"Father," said Wesley, "that's not true. Keenan—"

"What the hell do you know about it?" shouted Phillip. "You Christer."

"Father," said Keenan, "it's not true that I deliberately left you off the invitation list, but now that you're here, I won't have you cursing my brother in this company and in my fiancé's home."

"Your brother? My son."

"It's not necessary to defend me, Keenan," said Wesley.

Katherine stepped back in. "Mr. Garret, Father," she said, "would you accept a glass of brandy from me?"

"By way of peace offering?" said Phillip. "By God, yes. You have better sense than two of my sons with their heads put together."

Phillip quieted down some with a glass of brandy in his hand. He sat down to drink. Now and then he said something, but for the most part, he was a minor inconvenience in the crowd. Well, some people could tell and others could not, but Phillip had already consumed a goodly amount of brandy before making his way to Katherine's house. And after he had been served four more glasses, his head dropped. He was passed out completely. Wesley stepped outside to see if he could find out how Phillip had come to the house, and he found old Jacob outside waiting patiently with the buggy.

"Jacob," he said.

"Mr. Wesley."

"Father has passed out inside. I'll bring him out to you."

"Yes sir."

Wesley went back inside and got Keenan to help him lug Phillip out to the carriage. Jacob drove off with him then. Everyone in the house was greatly relieved.

The Medicine Man

♦ ♦ ♦

Skylar saddled his horse, and, leaving Charley Fox at his cabin in Webber's Falls, rode north. He had directions to the house of William Bear's Mouth. He had gotten the directions, along with a recommendation, from Gray Mouse. He had never met Bear's Mouth, a great and famous medicine man, one who could, it was said, make himself invisible or put his soul into the body of an owl or some other creature. He could read on a person and tell things about him, about his future even. Skylar felt a great need to meet this man and talk to him.

It was a long ride that took most of the day, and when he at last arrived at the small cabin in the woods, he was not at all certain that he had come to the right place. He turned his horse and rode slowly toward the cabin. When he drew closer, he could see a man standing on the porch leaning on a post that held up the roof. He rode closer still, and he could see that the man was a big man, powerful looking, with a full gray beard and not much hair on top of his head. The man was smiling. Skylar rode up to a hitching post, dismounted and tied his horse. He walked toward the man.

He was about to speak, when the big man beat him to it. "'Siyo, Skylar Garret," he said. "I've been expecting you."

Skylar was startled by that, even though he had often heard it said of medicine people that they knew when someone was coming. Instead of asking the question that was in his mind, he said, "'Siyo. You are William Bear's Mouth?"

"I am. Come in the house."

Skylar followed Bear's Mouth into the cabin and waited until the medicine man had indicated to him a chair. He sat down. Bear's Mouth poured two cups of coffee and handed one to Skylar. Then he sat down. He sipped his coffee, then put the cup down. He picked up a tobacco pouch and a pipe. "Captain Garret," he said, "do you have a pipe?"

Skylar fumbled in his pockets. "Yes," he said, and he pulled one out of a coat pocket.

Bear's Mouth reached toward him with the tobacco pouch. Skylar took it and filled his pipe bowl, then handed it back. Bear's Mouth filled his pipe. Then he found a match and struck it.

He lit his own pipe and then lit Skylar's. They sat for a moment and puffed, nearly filling the small room with smoke.

"You live in Webber's Falls," said Bear's Mouth.

"Yes. I do."

"And just now you have a young Cherokee boy staying with you."

"Yes. His name is Charley Fox."

"You have come to see me with a problem?"

"I, uh, well, I don't know if I should call it a problem or not. I have some questions I would like to have answered."

"Tell me."

"My father is a white man, and a very bad man. His name is Phillip Garret. My mother was Cherokee of the Wolf Clan. She died when I was little. She had money, and she owned their house in Fort Smith. She left it all to me, but my father refuses to admit it. He won't give me my money or my house. How can I make him turn it over to me?"

"Hmm."

"And then there is a woman, a Cherokee woman. I am in love with her and want to marry her, but my wicked father is also pursuing her. What should I do about that?"

"Captain Garret," said Bear's Mouth, "I have to check into all of this. I have to look into my crystal. I'll have some answers for you in four days. Come back then. And bring a fresh pouch of tobacco when you come."

"Wado," said Skylar. He had but few words of Cherokee. He stood up and walked to the door. Bear's Mouth sat and watched him. Skylar headed back toward his horse, as Bear's Mouth stood up and went to a back room in his cabin where he found a bag and opened it. He pulled out a large crystal and sat down with it.

As Skylar rode back toward Webber's Falls, he thought about his brief meeting with Bear's Mouth. *To hell with the teachers and preachers at the mission,* he thought. *To hell with their damned Christian religion. This is the kind of religion I can live with. This will sustain me. These are the beliefs of my mother and of her mothers.*

He began to feel more and more like an old Wolf Clan warrior. He was ready to kill and to take scalps. He felt like stripping off his clothes and painting his skin. He was suddenly very grateful to Mouse for sending him to Bear's Mouth. It was as if his whole life was changed and changed for the better. He knew that he would never again be the same Skylar Garret. His mother had given him a Cherokee name, but he could not recall it. He had been much too young when she died. He wondered if Mouse would remember it. He promised himself that he would ask Mouse the next time he saw him.

It all of a sudden became very important to him to have that name. He wondered if Bear's Mouth knew it or could find it in his crystal. He should have asked. *God damn it,* he said to himself, *why did I not ask?*

When he reached his cabin he could find no sign of Charley Fox. He rode around the settlement looking for him. He asked people if they had seen the boy. No one had. Charley's horse was gone too, so the boy must have ridden away for some reason. Perhaps after all he had decided to go back to Fort Smith and kill the rest of the white boys who had picked on him. He went back to the cabin and unsaddled his horse and went inside. He looked around for any evidence there might be, and it was then that he noticed that there was but one revolver where he had left two. He had thought that he should not be carrying his guns to the home of the medicine man, so he had left them behind. Now it appeared that the boy had taken one of them. "Oh, shit," he said.

Part of him said that he should go out looking for the boy, more seriously than he had looked before. Another part said that he should just stay home and forget about it. It was none of his business, after all. He was glad that his brother Wesley was not around. Wesley would have nagged him about his Christian responsibility toward the Cherokee boy. He didn't need that. He thought about Wesley. He loved Wesley, even though he was but a half brother and a white man. In spite of Wesley's religious beliefs, Wesley was a good man. Skylar was convinced of that. He berated himself for not having left Charley Fox with Wesley.

He tried to push Charley and Wesley out of his mind. He had much more important things to deal with just at that moment. His name was one, and the medicine man was another.

I renounce God.

♦ ♦ ♦

It was another couple of days when Skylar went back to Fort Smith and stopped by his father's house. He found Keenan and Wesley seated with the old man at the table with the brandy bottle in their midst. Each man had a glass in front of him. When Skylar stepped in, Phillip yelled out for the Stinker to bring another glass. Stinker complied quickly and a glass of brandy was poured for Skylar. The other three glasses were topped off. Wesley insisted that Stinker sit down with them and have a glass for himself.

"So," said Skylar, "what's the latest news in Fort Smith?"

"Ha," said Phillip, "they killed that little savage murderer that Wesley was so taken with."

"What?" said Skylar. "Are you talking about Charley?"

"Yes, he is, unfortunately," said Wesley. "The sheriff discovered his identity and went out with a posse looking for him. They had ridden out of Fort Smith

125

toward the Cherokee Nation, and they spotted him riding in this direction. They had one of the white boys with them that they figured were his targets. The white boy called out that was him, and they commenced to shooting without any warning. The body was riddled with bullets, they said. I should have kept him with me."

"You mean in my house?" said Phillip. "I'd have turned him in myself."

Wesley gave Phillip a hard look, picked up his glass and took a gulp of brandy.

"Why would you have done that?" said Skylar. "The whole affair was none of your business."

"The whole business of the whole human race is my business," said Phillip.

"I wish I could believe you, Father," said Wesley.

"Stop talking nonsense, Wesley," said Skylar.

"It's not nonsense," said Wesley. "That's the way it should be. We should all be our brother's keepers."

"Ha," said Keenan, "we're all doing well to be our own keepers without trying to be our brother's keepers or the keepers of the whole world. We're a sorry race, the human race. We should all be hanged."

"And if we were all hanged, Brother," said Skylar, "who would be the executioner?"

"Perhaps Wesley's God could do it."

"But Wesley's God just looks on in wonderment at the antics of his sorriest creation. He does not interfere with human activity. Isn't that right, Wesley?"

"I'm afraid it is."

"What kind of a God is that?" said Keenan. "You mean he is all powerful and all knowing, and he just

126

watches while murders and other atrocities are committed on a daily basis, while wars rage and horrible natural disasters occur killing thousands, including women and innocent, helpless children? What kind of a heartless God is that? And yet you say that God is Love. How can that be?"

"I can't explain it," said Wesley. "All I know is that I believe." *But in my heart*, he thought, *I do not know even that. I do not know if I really believe. Why did God let Charley be killed? I cannot reconcile that. I cannot accept it. God is cruel to allow that to happen.*

"You are a fool, little brother," said Skylar.

"You should have seen the body," said Phillip, "all riddled with bullet holes, all bloody. The blood caked with dirt where the bleeding carcass fell and rolled on the ground. A ghastly, horrible expression on the boy's brown and savage face. Ah, you should have seen it. It was a sight to behold."

"Damn it," shouted Wesley, frightening himself, "I renounce God, with all my heart."

They all sat in astonishment, staring at Wesley, unbelieving, almost horrified at what he had said. Even Skylar was startled, he who should have been pleased at Wesley's unexpected outburst. At last, Phillip picked up the brandy bottle and poured drinks all around. Wesley grabbed his up with enthusiasm and gulped it down. Phillip refilled it. They sat in silence for several moments, occasionally sipping some brandy. At last Skylar broke the quiet.

"Father," he said, "did my mother give me a Cherokee name when I was born?"

"What? What kind of a fool question is that to ask me?"

"I don't know anyone who might be able to answer it."

"If your savage mother had given you a savage name, she wouldn't have told it to me," said Phillip. "Your name is Skylar Romulus Garret. That's more than you deserve. If I could do it, I would have that taken away from you."

"You are an old son of a bitch," said Skylar.

"You see?" said Phillip, animated. "You see how he talks to his own father?"

"A father only in name," said Skylar, "and only by an accident of biology."

"I found you in the slop pot after your mother took a shit," said Phillip. "If I'd had any sense I would have emptied the whole load into the river, but like a fool I let her dig you out and save you."

"And one of these days, I will kill you, you old reprobate."

"That's enough of that, both of you," said Wesley. "You're going to drive me mad."

"Yes," said Keenan, "we're all family. Let's not quarrel among ourselves."

"All family?" said Stinker, finally breaking his long silence.

"Yes," said Wesley. "All of us. You included."

An Early Morning Message

♦ ♦ ♦

The next morning, early, a message came for Skylar, but Skylar was still sleeping it off. Stinker, who had not had as much to drink as the rest, was up and answered the door. He took the message for Skylar. He was tempted to open it and read it, if only to discover who had sent it, but he resisted. He checked Skylar's room but found Skylar sound asleep. Well, it would wait, he guessed. He went to the kitchen and made some coffee. He sat down and waited for it to percolate. When it was at last done, he poured himself a cup and sat down with it in Phillip's chair. He felt pompous sitting in Phillip's place and sipping his coffee. He liked it in the house when no one else was around. Well, they were all around, but they were all asleep.

He had finished two cups before he heard a noise in the house. Footsteps. He picked up his cup and poured himself another cup full. Then he sat down in a different chair and waited.

Soon, Keenan walked in and sat down. "You have some coffee?" he asked.

"Yes," said Stinker. "You want some?"

"Of course, I do," said Keenan. "Fetch me a cup."

Stinker went back to the pot and poured another cup, which he brought out to Keenan. He set the cup on the table in front of his half-brother. He felt resentful at Keenan's attitude.

Wesley never treated him that way. Nor did Skylar. Phillip, of course, treated him worse. He hated his father. Of course, he was far from alone in that feeling. Skylar hated the old man with a terrible hatred. Stinker knew that. Everyone knew it. He wasn't at all sure about Keenan's feelings toward Phillip, or toward much of anything, and he did not think that Wesley actually hated the old man. He might, but he fought against it. He was too much churchy to hate anyone. And finally, he thought that almost everyone in Fort Smith who knew Phillip would be pleased to see him dead.

He sipped his coffee, looking up from behind the cup at Keenan. Keenan sipped at his coffee. He looked surly, Stinker thought, but then, he wondered what he looked like himself.

He certainly felt surly. Then he said, for no reason that he could think of, "I've got a message for Skylar."

"A message?" said Keenan. "From whom?"

"I don't know. It's sealed."

"Where did you get it?"

"Someone brought it to the door early this morning."

"Do you still have it?"

"I'm waiting for him to wake up."

"Well, open it up. It might be something important."

"Important enough to wake him?"

"You never know. Break the seal."

Stinker had been wanting to do just that. Now that he had encouragement from Keenan, he felt bold enough to do it. He got up and walked to the sideboard where he had deposited the missive. He picked it up and walked back to the table. He sat down and held the message in front of him.

"Well," said Keenan, "what are you waiting for?"

"Nothing," said Stinker. He boldly broke the wax seal and unfolded the paper. He read quickly. Then he folded it up again.

"What is it?" said Keenan. "Who is it from?"

"It's Skylar's private business," said Stinker, tucking the folded paper underneath his vest.

Keenan sprang to his feet and rushed over to Stinker's side. "Damn you," he said, as he reached under Stinker's vest to retrieve the note. He pulled it out and unfolded it to read.

"Aha," he said, "it's from Adaline. She's invited him to a small gathering of friends at her house tomorrow night."

"That's none of my business and none of yours," said Stinker.

"Get a candle and melt the wax," said Keenan. "Reseal it."

Stinker found a candle and a match and lit the candle. Carefully he held the paper with the broken wax seal

131

over the flame, and when the wax was soft enough, he put the paper on the table and bashed the wax with the heel of his hand. "There," he said, "it's sealed again."

He sat back down to his coffee, placing the message on the table in front of him. Wesley came into the room. "Good morning, Brothers," he said.

"Would you like some coffee?" said Stinker, starting to stand up.

"Thank you," said Wesley. "I'll get it."

Stinker sat back down in his chair and gave Keenan a contemptuous look. Phillip came staggering in about then and sat down heavily in his chair. Without waiting for any word from Phillip, Stinker went for a cup of coffee which he placed on the table in front of Phillip. Phillip picked up the cup and sipped from it. He put it back down and made a face. "It's not good," he said. "A little brandy will improve it." Stinker got the brandy bottle and placed it before Phillip, who picked it up, uncorked it, and poured a healthy splash into his coffee. He took a drink. "Ah," he said. "That's better."

"Good morning, Father," said Wesley.

"Hmph," snorted Phillip, and then his eyes lit on the message in front of Stinker. "What the hell is that?" he said.

"What?" said Keenan.

"What? What indeed? That God damned paper in front of the bastard."

"Oh," said Stinker, picking up the paper. "This?"

"Yes, yes, that," said Phillip. "What is it?"

"It's just a message that came early this morning for Skylar," Stinker said.

"Who sent it?"

"I, uh, I don't know. It's sealed."

"Let me have it."

Stinker passed the note to Phillip, who looked at the messy wax seal and then tore the paper open. He read quickly and snorted. "From Adaline, huh. She must be planning to tell him that she's finished with him. The little party at her house is early enough. She'll send them all away in time."

"In time for what?" said Keenan.

"Why, she's coming here to see me tomorrow night," Phillip said. He grinned a lecherous grin, showing nasty yellow teeth with green on them here and there. "I invited her."

"That doesn't mean she'll come," said Keenan.

"She'll come. She'll be here all right. And we'll be married."

The Visitation

◆ ◆ ◆

Wesley went to his room that night and settled down in bed. He was restless, but finally he went to sleep, a fitful sleep. He tossed and turned. At last he heard someone call his name. "What?" he muttered. "Who is there?" Still he was asleep. "Wesley, my son," came the voice again. This time he sat up, or so he thought. He opened his eyes and stared into the darkness of the room. Gradually he saw a figure standing across the room. "I heard you that time you renounced the Lord." Wesley squinted his eyes. He stared hard at the figure in the dark room. The face seemed to light up. It became clear and was almost luminous. It was Reverend Wright. Wesley came up out of the bed and moved toward the apparition. "Reverend," he said, and his voice expressed adoration. "Reverend, you're here."

"I came to see you, my son. You're in need. You've lost your way. I've come to help."

"Oh, Reverend, have mercy on me."

"Why did you say what you said?"

"Terrible things have happened, Reverend. I cannot reconcile them with my beliefs."

"What things have happened?"

"I met a young boy, a Cherokee boy who was being bullied by white students in school. I tried to befriend him. He got hold of a gun somewhere and killed one of the boys. He threatened to kill the others. He went home with Skylar, and someone figured out who had done the shooting. A posse went after him and killed him."

"I'm sorry for that, my son."

"That's not the worst. It's my family."

"Tell me about them."

"They almost rejoiced in the boy's death. They told me how many bullet holes were in the poor body. They were horrible, and they're my relatives. I have the same evil blood running through my veins."

"You are you, my son. You are not your brothers or your father."

"I am my brother's keeper, and the sins of the father are visited upon the children."

"There are limits to both of those statements, my son. If you lead a good and righteous life, you do not have to worry about what your father may have done, and if your brother commits evil, you will not suffer from it."

"It's worse than that, Reverend."

"How is it worse?"

"I myself have my doubts. I feel as if I am as wicked as the rest of my family. I doubt my beliefs. I suspect myself. I want strong drink, and I want to commit evil."

"Wesley, you are allowing your doubts to overcome your better judgment. You are so good, that if you have a small doubt, you let that make you believe that you are an evil person. My son, everyone has doubts now and then. A good man must live through them and live in spite of them. Continue to live a good life."

"But I..."

"If a man spits on you, you may feel as if you would like to kill him. But you do not do so. If your eyes light on a beautiful woman, your mind may tell you that you would like to ravish her, but you keep still. Those are but the tribulations every man must face in this life. Do not let those kinds of feelings shake your faith."

"Reverend, if God is good and if he is all-powerful, how can he look down on the cruel things that happen in this world and allow them to go on?"

"He has made us in his image, and he has endowed us with free will. It is left to us if we will do good or evil. And then the formula is complicated by the actions of the Devil, who is in our midst and working all of the time against our Lord."

"Then I cannot believe in God if I do not also believe in the Devil?"

"That's correct. You must believe in the Devil in order to resist his evil machinations. He has the power to tempt you mightily. He takes advantage of your weaknesses, of your doubts, or your other temptations, and he tells you that you do not believe. He tells you there is no God, or that God is not all good or all powerful. He tells you that if your father is evil then you too are evil. He tells you that if your brothers feel thus and such way, then you too must feel that way. He is constantly at work on you, against you, and you must be constantly on your guard against him."

"How do I know if he is here?"

"Just know that he is here. He is always here. He can take on any form to fool you."

"Could he take on your form, Reverend?"

"He could."

"Then how can I know whether I am talking with you right now or if I am speaking with the Devil?"

"Your faith must let you know."

"Reverend, I don't know. I just don't know. I need an answer."

"I cannot give you one. It must come from your own heart and your conscience."

Skylar went to the home of Adaline and found a party already in progress. There was whiskey and brandy in abundance. There were prominent people there. There was laughing and dancing. When Adaline saw Skylar come into her house, she abandoned a dancing partner and rushed into his arms.

"Sky," she said. "My Skylar, I'm so glad that you're here. Dance with me, my darling."

They danced to the music of a guitar, a banjo and a fiddle. They shook the house. Skylar kissed her passionately. "My father said you were coming to him tonight," he said.

"He lied," she said, and she laughed. Skylar loved the sound of her laughter. It reminded him of waterfalls, or sometimes of rain lightly falling on a pond. He walked her to a couch and sat down with her. He began kissing her all over. She responded a bit, but she resisted when he became too ardent.

"What's wrong with you, my love?" he asked her.

"There are too many people here," she said.

"To hell with them," Skylar said.

"But I don't want them watching us."

"Then send them away, or I will do it for you. Just give me the word."

He stood up, and she pulled him back down by his arm. "No," she said. "I invited them here to my home for this party. It would be rude to tell them to leave."

Another man stepped up close to the couch. He was a stranger to Skylar. He was dressed in a black suit and sported two sidearms. He wore a drooping black mustache. He looked down at Adaline ignoring the presence of Skylar. "Dance with me," he said, and he took her by the hand and pulled her to her feet. Skylar sprang to his feet to confront the unwelcome interruption.

"Back off," he said. "The lady and I are talking."

" You've talked long enough," said the man. "I want a dance with her."

"You won't get it."

"We'll see about that."

"Get out of here now," said Skylar. "You're not wanted here any longer."

The man gave Skylar a terrific shove on the chest, knocking him down in a sitting position on the couch so hard that the couch went over backwards. Skylar got quickly to his feet and braced himself for a fight. The musicians stopped playing. Everyone else stopped talking. All laughter stopped. Everyone stared at Skylar and the stranger, anticipating violence.

"Gentlemen," said Adaline. "I'll have no fighting in my house."

"Then let's take it outside," said the stranger.

"With pleasure," said Skylar. He unbuttoned his coat as he walked out the door, to free up his two shoulder pistols. His opponent was wearing his pair on his hips. They stepped off the porch down into the yard, and the stranger said, "Are you ready?" Not waiting for a response, his right hand reached for the six-gun at his right side. Skylar pulled his gun from the left side of his chest with his right hand, and his gun flashed and roared. The stranger looked horribly surprised. His knees bent slightly. His gun was in his hand out of the holster but only raised about halfway up. He swayed a bit, and then he fell over backward and landed with a thud on the hard ground.

Skylar stood holding his smoking revolver in his hand, looking down at the bleeding body. He sneered and said out loud, "God damned bastard white man."

Adaline had come running out of the house, followed by all of her guests. She stood for a moment at the edge of her porch looking at the results of the recent altercation. Then she rushed down into the yard and threw her arms around Skylar.

"Oh, Sky," she said. "My Skylar, you've killed him."

"Who was he?" Skylar asked.

"He was an old acquaintance of mine," she said. "I hadn't seen him for years until tonight."

"Did he have a name?"

"Archie," she said. "Archibald Torrance. He had been an officer in the army."

"Ha," he said. "So had I."

"When the law shows up, Adaline," Skylar said, "tell them the truth. That man went for his gun first. I shot him in self-defense. That's the whole story." He went for his horse with Adaline clinging to his arm. "I have to go now," he said. "Let go of me."

"I'll go with you," she said, still crying. "Take me with you."

Skylar flung his arm to get loose from Adaline, but he flung it much too hard. She went flying away from him and fell in the yard. She screamed a short shrill scream. "You bastard," she said.

"Yes," he said, swinging up into the saddle, "I'm a Garret. Remember. Tell them the truth."

He spurred his horse and raced away, turning to go in the direction of Webber's Falls in the Cherokee Nation. He was riding fast, too fast for the distance he was going to travel.

The Murder

♦ ♦ ♦

Phillip waited anxiously in the certain knowledge, so he thought, that Adaline would be there. He had three thousand dollars to show her, or to give her, whatever it would take to get her to the altar with him in the morning. She would be his next wife. He was sure of it. He needed another wife, a young and beautiful one. She would keep him young. He had thought that he would not drink until after she came, but the waiting was more than he could take. He poured himself a brandy and tossed it down quickly. It was so good that he poured another and then another. He was beginning to be wobbly on his feet.

He heard a knock on his door, and his heart suddenly raced. He hurried to the door as fast as his uncertain legs would carry him, and with a big smile on his wretched old face, he threw the door wide open. The smile dropped. His expression changed to one of disappointment and then of anger. "What the hell are you doing in here?" he snarled.

Skylar shoved past him and moved into the room. "Be careful how you speak to me," he said. "I've just killed a man tonight."

"What?"

"He was a white man, like you."

"God damn you," said Phillip. "What have you done?"

"I just told you. I killed a white man."

"The law will be after you," said Phillip.

"I've come for some of my money."

"You have no money. I've told you that. You owe me money."

"You lying old reprobate. Give me my money. I'll kill you."

To reassure himself, Phillip reached up and clutched his bathrobe at his left breast. His three thousand dollars was secured just inside the robe. He felt it there. He hoped he had not given himself away by that move, but Skylar had not noticed it. Skylar reached instead inside his own coat and pulled out a revolver which he pointed at the old man's chest. "I said I'll kill you," he said. He cocked the revolver and stretched out his arm. Phillip trembled. "Give me my money," said Skylar.

Old Jacob was lying in his bed in the small house next door. He was not asleep. He had not been able to go to sleep, although he had been in bed for at least an hour. He was suddenly startled by the loud report of a gun. It sounded to him as if it were just next door in the main house. He jumped up, and in his night shirt, put on his slippers. He hurried to the door and jerked it open. Then he started running to the main house. He rounded the corner of the big house and came face to face with Skylar, whose eyes were wide.

Skylar was about as startled as was old Jacob. He raised his right hand, still holding the revolver high over his head, and he brought it back down hard and sudden and bashed the old man's head. Jacob dropped like a sack of flour. Skylar ran.

Upstairs in the main house, the shot aroused both Wesley and Keenan from their slumber. They came running down the stairs almost together. Hurrying into their father's room, they saw the bloody body immediately. Its head was bashed in horribly. He was obviously dead.

"Skylar," said Wesley, a ghastly look on his face.

"No," said Keenan. "Not Skylar."

"If we hurry out, we might catch him," said Wesley.

"Whoever he is," said Keenan. "Let's go."

They hurried outside. They saw no sign of a culprit. No sign of Skylar. They were about to go back in when they spotted old Jacob lying by the corner of the house. They rushed to his side and Keenan lifted his head. "He's alive," he said. "Let's get him into the house."

They washed the blood from Jacob's head and bound the head with a clean rag. Jacob moaned.

"Oh," he said, "where am I?"

"We brought you into the house, Jacob," said Keenan. "Who did this to you?"

"It was Mister Skylar," Jacob said. "Mister Skylar."

Wesley and Keenan looked at one another for a moment in silence. Then Keenan said, "Watch over him, Wesley. I'll saddle a horse and go for the law."

As Keenan was hurrying toward the door, Wesley called out, "And a doctor."

"A doctor," said Keenan. "Yes. Of course."

When Skylar reached the Cherokee Nation, he did not stop at Webber's Falls. He turned north and kept riding until he arrived at the home of Bear's Mouth. When he rode up to the house, as late as it was, he saw the medicine man standing on the porch with a smile on his face. Dismounting, Skylar said,

"Siyo, Bear's Mouth."

"Welcome back, Skylar Garret," said the medicine man.

There were two straight chairs standing on the porch by the front door. The medicine man indicated the chairs and said, "Sit down." Skylar sat down in one and Bear's Mouth in the other. "I've been waiting for you here," said Bear's Mouth."

"I, uh, I was detained in Fort Smith," said Skylar. "It was unavoidable."

The medicine man leaned over to his left and picked up a pouch from the porch. "Smoke this in the morning about sunrise. Smoke it again before lunch and again at night after the sun has gone down. It will take care of all your problems."

"How long must I keep this up?"

"Until all of the tobacco is used up."

Skylar thanked Bear's Mouth and left. He had not told Bear's Mouth about the incident at the Garret House. It had not seemed important to him. The business with his family was one thing. His business with Bear's Mouth was something else. But he had also not asked the medicine man about his Cherokee name, and that was something he had intended to do. But he had the doctored tobacco, and not much else was in his head at the moment.

The Arrest

♦ ♦ ♦

As Skylar rode up to his house, he saw two white men lounging in front of his house. Their horses were tied in the yard. When he drew even closer, he saw the badges on their chests. His first instinct was to run, but he thought better of it. Bear's Mouth had given him medicine and told him that it would solve all his problems. He pulled his horse up beside the other two and dismounted. "Hello," he said. "What can I do for you?"

"Are you Skylar Garret?" said one of the men.

"I am."

"I'm Deputy U.S. Marshal Toby Smith," said the man. "This is Deputy Thompson. We're here to arrest you for murder."

Skylar walked over to the men and opened his coat to reveal his two Army Colts. Smith took them.

"I'll give you no trouble," said Skylar. "It was not a murder, and I will be acquitted. May I take time for a smoke?"

The deputies looked at one another. Thompson shrugged. Smith said, "Go ahead. I see no problem."

Skylar took out the tobacco pouch he had gotten from Bear's Mouth and got his pipe from another pocket. He filled the pipe bowl, took a match out of his pocket and struck it. Then he puffed deeply on his pipe to get it going. His thoughts were a prayer for good things to come.

"I've ridden my horse a long ways tonight," he said. "Could we spend the night here and ride back to Fort Smith in the morning?"

"Why not?" said Thompson.

Already another pair of deputies were at the home of Phillip Garret, investigating the murder of that old man. Wesley, Keenan, Jacob and Stinker were there. The deputies studied the body carefully and the surrounding room. There was not much evidence of any kind of a struggle in the room or anywhere else in the house or on the grounds. It did not take long, however, to see that the old man had not been shot. His head had been bashed in, possibly with the butt of a revolver. Jacob said that his own head had been bashed with a revolver. He had survived. He was lucky.

"The old man had three thousand dollars on him," said Jacob.

"Three thousand?" said the deputy who called himself Jackson. His partner, known as Durham, said, "That's a good motive for murder."

"All we have to do is figure out who done it," said Jackson.

"It was Mister Skylar," said Jacob. "He's the one."

"Skylar?" said Jackson.

"That's my brother," said Keenan, "Skylar Garret."

"He's been heard to threaten our father's life numerous times," said Wesley.

"I heared the gunshot," said Jacob, "and I jumped out a my bed in the house next door and come a-running, but as I was coming around the corner a the house, this house, that is, I run right smack into him."

"Into who?" said Jackson.

"Mister Skylar," said Jacob. "He was a-running away from the house, and he had a gun in his hand."

"What kind of gun?" asked Jackson.

"A gun," said Jacob. "What do I know from guns? It was a gun."

Jackson drew out his big Colt .45 and held it out for Jacob to see. "Was it like this?"

"It were jist like that," Jacob said.

Jackson holstered his weapon. "Go on," he said.

"Well, that's about all. He raised up that big gun and brung it down on top a my poor ole head. That's all I know. I don't know nothing after that til I woke up in bed. Mister Wesley and Mister Keenan brung me in here, I reckon. Leastwise, I seen them first when I come to."

Durham turned to the two brothers. "Where did you find Jacob?" he asked.

"Just outside by the corner of the house," said Keenan.

"What took you there?"

"We heard the shot. We were sleeping upstairs. We ran down and found Father there. Then we ran out, thinking we might see the culprit. We found Jacob lying there bloody. We brought him inside."

"Come and show me where you found him," said Durham. They went outside, and the brothers showed Durham where they had discovered Jacob. There was a bit of blood on the ground there. The deputies looked around some more, but they found nothing of interest. Then Keenan reminded them that Jacob had identified Skylar as his assailant.

"There ain't much doubt about it," said Jackson.

"Yeah," said Durham. "We got to find Skylar Garret and arrest him."

"Or kill him," said Jackson.

"Let's go back to the courthouse and tell the judge," said Durham.

Jackson and Durham obtained a warrant for the arrest of Skylar Garret. They were walking out of the courthouse headed for their horses when they met Thompson and Smith with Skylar in chains, walking into the courthouse. The courthouse was a huge brick building sitting on top of the prison. The prison was where Thompson and Smith were headed with Skylar. "Howdy, boys," said Jackson. "What you got there?"

"Fella name of Garret," said Smith. "He done a killing."

"Not Skylar Garret?" said Jackson, looking at the warrant in his hand.

"That's the one," said Smith.

"That's who we was going after," said Jackson. "Killed his own daddy. I reckon he'll hang, all right."

"I will not hang, you oafs," said Skylar, "but did I hear you right? Has my father been killed?"

"As if you didn't know," said Jackson. "You bashed his head in last night, and you'll hang for it."

"I will not, for I am innocent, but I'm glad the old man is dead."

"That kind of talk won't help your case any," said Durham.

"Nevertheless, I am glad of the news."

The Evidence Piles Up

♦ ♦ ♦

That night Skylar sat alone in his cell considering his situation. He was not worried about the killing of the stranger at Adaline's house. It was clear cut. He would be exonerated. There were witnesses to the fact that the man had pulled his gun first, and Skylar had only fired in self-defense. That was no problem. That was the reason he had come along so peacefully with the two deputies. It was the other killing that worried him. The killing of his father. He had heard enough from the second pair of deputies to know that the evidence was piling up against him. It was widely known that he hated his father. That in itself might be enough evidence against him. He had also bragged all over town that Phillip was living on his property and his money, and that he intended to get what he owned. He would get it if he had to kill his father for it. Plenty of people had heard him say as much. Finally, it was widely known that he and his father both

155

were pursuing Adaline with marriage in mind. Clearly, there was sufficient evidence to hold him for a trial, and if he were found guilty, he would hang. Well, he decided, he would deserve it. He was guilty. There was no doubt about that.

He had regrets. He still longed for the soft touch of Adaline's body. He wanted to grow old alongside her, to have children with her, perhaps even live long enough to see grand-children and watch them grow. He wondered what he would look like with a full head of white hair, and he wondered what his health would be like in his old age. He would like to make his fortune. But he was thinking like a white man, he realized. And he was not a white man. He was Cherokee.

He had his medicine from Bear's Mouth, and it was supposed to protect him against all odds. Things would work out for him for the best. He believed in the Cherokee medicine. He believed in the old medicine man. He trusted him, but Bear's Mouth had not known about the killing of old Phillip. Or had he? He did not mention it, but Skylar knew that the old man could see things. Perhaps he did know.

Perhaps the medicine would protect Skylar even against this charge.

Keenan had not realized just how much he loved his brother until Skylar had been arrested for murder. Now he was worried. The evidence against Skylar was overwhelming. It was frightening to think about. Right after the shot had been fired, Jacob had run into Skylar fleeing from the scene, and Skylar had struck him on the head. And an examination of the body had shown that Phillip had been killed in just that same way. His head had been bashed in. There was other evidence, some of it circumstantial. Keenan was indeed afraid for the safety of his brother.

But Keenan was further surprised. He had to admit to himself that he was glad that old Phillip was dead. It was about time, he thought. Why had Skylar waited so long? The old man had needed to be killed, if ever a man needed such a thing. If it had not been for the situation that Skylar was in, Keenan would have been rejoicing in his father's untimely death. He had been a wretched old heathen, a reprobate, a scoundrel and he had certainly deserved his miserable fate.

But Wesley had a different reaction entirely. He was sorry for Skylar, of course, for he, like Keenan, had come to love his brother. But while he loved him, he mourned for his soul, for Skylar had a wicked soul. Wesley knew that. Skylar's wicked soul had influenced even Wesley's own, had made Wesley doubt his own faith, and he would surely have been lost at that moment had not Reverend Wright come to visit him in the night. Wesley was afraid that his brother Skylar might be hanged. He certainly did not want that to happen, but if it did, it would all be for the best. For Skylar was guilty of a most horrible crime, and all Wesley could do was pray.

Wesley went down the stairs and found Keenan and the Stinker sitting at the table drinking brandy. The

Stinker was sitting in old Phillip's chair, and he was dressed up nicely in some of Phillip's finest clothes. Wesley was almost startled. He had never before realized just how nearly Stinker and Phillip were to the same size. Stinker looked almost good, almost --handsome. Wesley said good morning to them and took a seat. He did not want any of the brandy. Instead, he asked, "Do you have coffee?"

Stinker said yes, and Wesley got up to pour him a cup.

"You look ready to travel, Brother," said Keenan.

"I'm riding over to the mission," said Wesley.

"I didn't think you had any reason to go there anymore," said Stinker, "now that your mentor has died."

"You mean Reverend Wright, I suppose," said Wesley.

"Of course," said Keenan. "Who else?"

"I haven't thought I had much reason for going there lately," Wesley said, "but all of a sudden, I feel a need to visit again."

"I suppose I can understand," said Keenan. "You likely feel a need to pray for our brother in a holy place surrounded by holy men. I doubt if you need that. I think you yourself are a holy man, Brother."

"I am not a holy man," said Wesley. "Far from it. Please do not say that again."

"As you wish, Brother," said Keenan.

Wesley finished his coffee and left the house.

The Benefactor

♦ ♦ ♦

Keenan went to the home of his soon to be wife. She invited him happily into her home.

"Keenan," she said, "I was so sorry to hear the dreadful news of your father's death and of the arrest of your dear brother, Skylar. Will they find him guilty of murder and hang him, do you think?"

"I am very much afraid so, Katherine," said Keenan. "The evidence is absolutely overwhelming."

"And do you think he is guilty?"

"He hated Father," said Keenan. "He believed that Father had control of his money and his property. He and Father were both after the same woman. He had been heard to threaten Father's life on many different occasions. Finally, when Jacob ran to investigate a shot in the main house, he ran right into Skylar who was running away from the house, and then bashed Jacob in the head, knocking him unconscious. I fear that he is guilty and must hang. But, no, I do not believe it. Something prevents me from believing it."

"How horrible," she said, "and to think, I might have married him."

"Don't ever think it," said Keenan. "You did not, and you are free to marry me. We must be wed as soon as possible, my darling."

"Yes, darling," she said, "right away. But Keenan."

"Yes?"

"Do you really believe Skylar to be a murderer?"

"No," he said. "I do not."

News of Phillip's death and of Skylar's arrest reached Gray Mouse, and he traveled to Fort Smith. He tried to think of some legal reason the trial should be moved to the Cherokee courts, but there was none. Skylar was a Cherokee citizen, but he was accused of killing a white man outside of the Cherokee Nation. Even if the killing had occurred in the Cherokee Nation, the U.S. would not allow the Cherokee courts to try a case involving a white man. So Skylar would be forced to endure the white man's court with the hanging judge Parker sitting on the bench.

Mouse wracked his brain for some way in which he could help his kinsman. There must be some way.

Bail money? A loaded pistol? What could he do? He had already recommended Bear's Mouth to Skylar.

He wondered if Skylar had gone to see the medicine man. He hoped that he had, for Mouse was convinced that Bear's Mouth's medicine could save Skylar. In fact, he himself had gone to see the old medicine man and told him about the murder and the arrest, and Bear's Mouth had told him that he would visit Skylar. He gave

Mouse something to take to Skylar, and he told Mouse that he had found out Skylar's Cherokee name. It was Noq'si. For the rest, Mouse would have to pray, long and hard. He could think of nothing else to do that was practical. He decided that at least he could visit his cousin in the jail.

He was sitting at a table in a roadside café drinking a cup of coffee and thinking hard about his cousin's problems. He did not believe that Skylar was guilty of the murder of Phillip, but even if he was, Mouse reasoned, there was really nothing wrong with it. Phillip Garret had been a man who, if anyone ever did, deserved to die. If Skylar had done the deed, then it should be called justifiable homicide, at the very least. Mouse would give him a medal if it were in his power.

Phillip may have been a murderer himself. There was the business of the mysterious early deaths of his wives and of the poor girl who was the mother of the Stinker. And then the way in which the old man had treated his own children, ignoring them and leaving them to be raised by old Jacob. They would never have been educated at all had it not been for Mouse. He had taken pity on them, first and especially his cousin Skylar, but once he had determined to take care of Skylar's education, he could not keep himself from taking pity on the other two, even though they were white boys and in no way related to him.

He had to find a way to help. He finished his coffee and got up. He headed for the Fort Smith prison. He decided that he would stop along the way and hire a good lawyer.

The Garret House

♦ ♦ ♦

Noq'si or Star, no longer Skylar, sat alone in his cell. He was grateful for the visit of his cousin Mouse who had told him his Cherokee name, having learned it from Bear's Mouth. He would never have given himself up so easily to the two damned white lawmen had he known that he was going to be charged with Phillip's murder. They had come for him for the killing of Archibald what the hell was his name, and that was a clear case of self defense. He had witnesses. But in the meantime, they had come up with evidence against him in the other killing. He figured that old Jacob must be all right or they would have charged him with that one as well. They could charge him, he realized, with assault against Jacob. He had damn sure done that, and he imagined that Jacob himself was a witness. And that could be called assault with a deadly weapon, for he had used his revolver even though he had not fired it.

He thought more about it and about all the evidence that would be brought to bear against him, and at last he decided that he must hang. There just was no way around it. And the more he thought about that, the more he convinced himself that he deserved it. He was too much like old Phillip. It hurt him to admit it, but damn it, it was so. That itself was enough to hang him for, but there was more. He had wanted Phillip dead, had wanted that badly. He would never deny that, not for any reason. Phillip had robbed him, and he deserved to die. And Star had wished him dead, and had threatened to kill him over and again. Yes, he concluded, if he were on the jury, he would vote guilty.

Keenan was back at the Garret house. He wanted some brandy, but he did not feel like drinking alone. In fact, Keenan never felt like drinking alone. He liked to drink, but only if he had some company.

There was no one in the dining area at the table where the brandy was kept. He went through the house looking for his brother the Stinker. At last he checked Phillip's bedroom and found Stinker there going through an old trunk.

"Well, Stinker," he said, "are you finding anything of interest?"

Stinker jumped and looked around. "Oh," he said, "you frightened me, Mister Keenan. No. Nothing of any real interest. Some old papers is all. Nothing of much interest. Well, Skylar, I guess, would find a few of them interesting."

"And why is that?"

"Well, now, Brother, I'm not much good at reading, but it looks like to me that this one here proves his claim that the house is really his."

"What?" shouted Keenan, running over to Stinker and grabbing the paper to study it. "By God, Stinker, you are absolutely right. This is Skylar's house."

Stinker chuckled. "Fat lot of good that'll do him now," he said.

"What do you mean by that, you scoundrel?"

"Well, he's going to hang, ain't he?"

"They haven't found him guilty yet, damn you, and I'm not convinced that he is guilty."

"You might be right about that, too, Brother," said Stinker. "Say, do you suppose he was right about the money too?"

"Let's look through all those papers and see what we can find."

"If he was right, what will happen to the money if they do hang him?"

"I don't know. I suppose the court will have to decide."

"We're his nearest relatives, ain't we?" said Stinker. "Who would have more right to it than us? I mean Wesley too, of course, although him being so godly and all, he might not want it."

"He might not," said Keenan.

"Keenan," said Stinker, "the court might decide that I'm not a real Garret and not entitled to a share. If you get the money, and I don't, will you share it with me?"

"Stinker, I believe all this discussion is a bit premature. We don't know if there's enough money to be worrying about, and we have no idea what the court will decide about it, if there's anything to decide. Skylar may be acquitted, you know."

"You ought to share it with me, Keenan. If it weren't for me none of this would be happening, you know."

"What are you talking about, Stinker?"

"It was me who killed the old man."

"You?"

"Yes. I did it."

Keenan backed away from Stinker until he backed into the table. Keeping his eyes on the Stinker, he felt for a chair and sat down. Still he stared as in disbelief. "Why?" he said.

"Do you think that Skylar was the only one who hated him? I hated him. He was mean to me. He was my father too, but he treated me like a slave. Even the slaves got freed, but not me. And then I heard Skylar suggest that the old fart had killed my mother. On top of all that, he had three thousand dollars tucked under his robe that night. Are those reasons enough for you?"

"I'd say they were pretty good reasons, Stinker, but Skylar ran out of here with a revolver in his hand and he struck Jacob down with it. We all heard a shot."

"I was in the kitchen when Skylar came in. I kept quiet and listened. He threatened the old man, demanded some money. The old man refused him, of course. Skylar became furious. He fired a shot over the old man's head and into the wall. The old man screamed, covered his head with his hands and fell down on his knees. I'm sure that he believed that he was about to be murdered. But for some reason, perhaps his own shot scared him, I don't know, but Skylar turned and ran out of the room.

"You and Wesley and old Jacob all heard the shot and came running, but I was faster. I ran into the bedroom and got old Phillip's revolver from where he kept it on his desk, and I quickly brained him, and then I reached under his robe and found the three thousand. I have it right here."

Stinker reached into a jacket pocket and pulled out the bills, holding them out to Keenan as if to prove that he was not lying.

Keenan looked at them but did not touch them. "Here," said Stinker, "take half of this money, and when the court gives you all the rest of old Garret's money, you can give me half. Okay? All right?"

"Get away from me, you dirty nigger," shouted Keenan. "I don't want your filthy money. I'm going to the police and tell them that you are the murderer, you and not Skylar."

"No. Don't do that. They won't believe you. They've already decided that he's guilty anyway. They're going to hang him just the same. Let's make some money out of all this."

The Wedding

♦ ♦ ♦

It was as big a wedding as Fort Smith could remember. It was too big for Katherine's house, so Keenan had asked Wesley if he could get permission for them to use the mission. Wesley had gotten permission, and so it was held in the chapel at the mission. No one brought up Keenan's atheism, and Keenan himself seemed to have repressed it temporarily for the sake of Katherine. The little chapel was crammed with guests. Judge Parker was there, as was General Arbuckle from Fort Gibson. Principal Chief W.P. Ross of the Cherokee Nation was present, along with his wife, as were the chiefs of the other of the five tribes.

There were local political personages from Fort Smith and council members from all of the five tribes.

The crowd was like a local who's who.

They stood around outside the chapel visiting with each other while they waited for the proper time to go inside for the ceremony. Some of the guests gossiped with one another about the irony of the judge being at

169

the wedding of Keenan Garret at about the same time as he was preparing to preside over the murder trial of Keenan's brother, Skylar. Others, more decorous, simply talked about the charms of Katherine and the gallantry of Keenan. A few spoke in near whispers of the close escape Katherine had gotten when she did not marry Skylar, and how much better off she was going to be with his brother.

And a few of the bolder, and perhaps more rude, guests spoke with one another of the recent murder of the groom's father.

At last they were summoned into the chapel, and when they were all seated, a woman of the mission sat down to play the organ. The organ had been recently acquired for the mission by the efforts of Reverend Wright, and the late reverend had been particularly proud of the instrument. He had confided to Wesley on one occasion that he was afraid that he was guilty of the sin of pride. The tune chosen by the organist was, of course, the wedding march. The crowd was seated and, at last, quiet. Keenan was in the front of the chapel with the same preacher who had preached the funeral sermon for Reverend Wright.

Wesley, seated somewhere in the center of the crowd, took note of that fact. It was a sad one to him.

At last, when the anticipation was just about more than anyone could longer bear, Katherine came walking in slowly, accompanied by Judge Parker. Wesley was surprised. He had not noticed that Parker was no longer a part of the crowd. He twisted his neck and looked around until he finally found Mrs. Parker seated alone.

That was quite a coup, he thought, for Katherine to have gotten the famous Hanging Judge to give her away. Who would ever have thought it? Even at her wedding, she was thinking about political, if not advancement, then at least advantage. Katherine was indeed a very clever woman. He would not allow himself to say that she was a schemer.

Finally the music stopped. It was quiet in the chapel. A few coughs were heard and some throat clearing. The preacher gave the standard lecture about marriage to the bride and groom, and he asked if anyone present had any reason that the ceremony should not proceed. No one did. So he continued reading from his book. Wesley caught himself looking at Katherine and trying to see through her clothing.

I am awful, he told himself, but he could not stop his mind from working on the problem. She was a beautiful bride, and underneath all that wedding finery, she must have been absolutely breath-taking. He found himself being envious of his brother. He longed for the ceremony to come to an end.

At last it did. "You may kiss the bride," the preacher said, and Keenan enfolded Katherine in his arms and pressed his lips to hers. Wesley thought that the kiss lasted much longer than was necessary.

The wedding was, after all, a mere public ceremony, and the kiss was only a part of that ceremony.

Wesley began questioning the reason for the ceremony, the use in having a preacher bless the union of man and woman who had already blessed it themselves. He had heard Skylar say that when Cherokees wanted to be married, they merely exchanged symbolic gifts and then went to a house together. Suddenly that made sense to Wesley.

The wedding ended, and the crowd went back to the main building of the mission where food was spread out over one long table top. The guests swarmed over it like so many hogs at a trough. Keenan and Katherine were cutting the large, ostentatious cake. Wesley looked for an opportunity to escape. He sidled to the front door, watched the crowd, and when he was certain that no one was looking his way, made a quick exit. Just outside, he stepped to the right of the door and leaned back on the wall to suck in some deep and heavy breaths.

The Zeke Proctor Case

◆ ◆ ◆

Wesley was thinking about murder trials. How did the members of a jury decide upon a man's guilt or innocence? Especially if there were no witnesses? In the case of his brother, the nearest thing to a witness was old Jacob, whose head had gotten bashed in, and Jacob could attest to the fact that Skylar had bashed his head but not that he had bashed Phillip's head in. That would be mere speculation. Would that be enough for a jury to condemn Skylar? Wesley thought that it should not be but was very much afraid that it might be.

He had heard in the murder cases that came before Judge Parker, that Parker had hand-picked jurors. In fact he had heard them called professional jurors, and it was strongly rumored that the judge carefully instructed them before the trial, and they would always vote the way he wanted them to vote. So if there were a way to get the judge on Skylar's side, Skylar would likely be set free. But how could that be done? Wesley had no idea.

He tried to recall other recent murder trials, but the only thing that came into his mind was the case of Zeke Proctor, and that case had never reached Parker's court. Wesley tried to think of some way in which the Zeke Proctor case might be instructive in Skylar's case, but he couldn't find any areas of comparison, other than the fact that Proctor and Skylar were both Cherokees.

He was seized by a sudden desire to visit the inn that straddled the border between the Cherokee Nation and Arkansas up at Shiloh, Arkansas. He got himself up and went downstairs. He was about to go outside, when his brother, Keenan, stopped him. "Where are you going, Wesley?"

"I'm riding up to Shiloh," said Wesley. "Go with me."

As they moved along the road going north, riding side by side, Keenan asked Wesley, "So why are we going up there?"

"I've been puzzling over an old murder trial," said Wesley. "The case of Zeke Proctor, a Cherokee."

"I've heard of it," said Keenan.

"Zeke had a sister who was married to a white man named Kesterson," said Wesley. "They lived down this way somewhere. Well, apparently Kesterson abandoned the woman and their two small children. By the time Zeke heard about it, they were nearly starved. He drove down from his home in the northern part of the Cherokee Nation in a wagon, and he got his sister and her children and took them home with him to care for them. That might have been the end of it, but Kesterson, not knowing when to leave well enough alone, moved in

174

with another Cherokee woman who lived in Zeke's own neighborhood."

"I'm not surprised that he got himself killed," said Keenan.

"But he did not," said Wesley. "Zeke went to this inn I want to visit. As I understand it, it's built right on top of the line, of the boundary between the Cherokee Nation and Arkansas, and inside there is a stripe painted down the center of the floor. If you're standing on one side of the room, you're in Arkansas, but if you step over the line, you're in the Cherokee Nation."

"Really?" said Keenan. "That must be strange."

"What is really strange about it is that you can purchase alcohol on the Arkansas side of the line and even sit down there and drink it, but if you dare to carry it across the line, you'll be in violation of the liquor laws of the Cherokee Nation and the United States."

"And you want to go there and drink on the Arkansas side?"

"I don't know, Keenan. I just want to visit the place. That's all. I'm sorry if I've taken you away from your new wife."

"That's all right, Wesley," Keenan answered, "I told her that I would be away for most of this day. I said that I would be looking into Skylar's case."

"As we probably both should be."

"But here now. You abandoned the story of Zeke Proctor when you started to describe the fascinating inn on the border."

"Oh, yes. Well, Zeke went to the inn and sat down on the Arkansas side of the room and ordered a drink of whiskey. He drank a few, no one knows how many, and the whole time he was thinking about that damned Kesterson. Finally he stood up and headed for the door. I imagine the storekeeper called out to him, something like, "Going so soon? You just got here." Zeke replied, "I'm going to kill myself a white man." He went to the mill where Kesterson was living with the woman, who was a Beck. The Becks and Proctors were both prominent Cherokee families, you know."

"Yes," said Keenan.

"So Zeke found Kesterson outside, and the Beck woman, too. He told Kesterson that he meant to kill him, and he pulled out his revolver. The Beck woman jumped in front of Kesterson just as Zeke fired his shot, and she was killed."

"So Zeke killed the woman and not Kesterson?"

"That's correct. Kesterson ran away. Zeke, upon determining that the woman was dead, went to the nearest Cherokee sheriff and told what he had done. I suppose the sheriff arrested him and released him on his own recognizance. A trial was scheduled, but one of the two families objected to something. I don't recall just what. The judge was related to someone, or the prosecutor or something. Anyway, they fought back and forth for a while before the trial was finally scheduled and no one objected any more.

In the meantime, Kesterson had gone to Fort Smith and filed charges against Zeke for attempting murder on a white man, himself. So a federal warrant was issued for Zeke Proctor. But the judge told the deputy marshals who had the warrant to attend the Cherokee trial and watch. If the Cherokee court found Zeke guilty of murder and sentenced him to hang, then all was well, but if by chance, they found him innocent or acquitted him, the deputies were to arrest him on the federal warrant."

"That's hedging your bets," said Keenan. "So how did it all turn out?"

"The day of the trial, everyone was there. A crowd had gathered. The Becks were the last to arrive, and when they started to enter the court room, Zeke's brother, whose name was Johnson, blocked the door, because the Becks were obviously heavily armed. Johnson was unarmed. One of the Becks shot Johnson dead. Then everyone started shooting. A number of people were killed. Zeke ran away. The Cherokee Nation issued warrants for the arrest of all the Becks who were there, and the U.S. court at Fort Smith issued warrants for the arrest of all the Proctors, including poor dead Johnson."

"It sounds totally insane," said Keenan. "What possible reason could there have been for issuing a warrant for the arrest of the dead brother? He had been unarmed and murdered."

"Zeke was hiding out with the Nighthawk Keetoowahs, and the officials at Fort Smith requested help in apprehending Zeke from the chief of the Cherokee Nation."

"Who was that? The chief?"

"It was Lewis Downing. He was himself a full-blood Cherokee and a member of the Nighthawk Keetoowas. The officials at Fort Smith were angry at his refusal and had just about decided to send for the army from Fort

Sill, when a cooler head prevailed and suggested that they issue a general amnesty, and that's what they did at last."

"My God, Brother. There might easily have been another Cherokee war."

"Yes, and our Skylar might have been fighting against the U.S. in it."

"He might indeed. He almost surely would have."

"I don't know why I've been so preoccupied with this case. It happened a few years ago, and it has nothing to do with Skylar's situation. I just can't help myself."

They reached the inn in question after several hours of traveling, and they tied their horses and went inside. The first thing they each noticed was the line that had been painted down the middle of the room.

Wesley was standing in Arkansas, and Keenan in the Cherokee Nation. A friendly enough man looked up and asked, "What can I do for you?"

Keenan pointed to a table with two chairs on the Arkansas side of the line and said to Wesley, "Do you want to sit down and have a drink?"

"Yes," said Wesley, "I would."

They sat down at that table and ordered two glasses of whiskey. When the man brought the drinks, Keenan said, "Were you here when Zeke Proctor left to kill Kesterson?"

"I sure was."

"Did you know where he was going?"

"Nope. Just knew he was going somewhere to kill some white man is all."

"That was a very strange case, wasn't it?"

"Sure was. Strangest I ever heared of. You know, Zeke finally went over into Arkansas and got hisself elected sheriff in one of them counties over there?"

"Is that right?" said Keenan. "Outlaw one day and lawman the next."

"That's the way it goes around these parts. Where you fellas from?"

"We're from Fort Smith," said Wesley.

"You've come a long ways for a drink," the man said.

"My brother here," said Keenan, "wanted to see the famous paint stripe down the middle of the room."

"Well, that there is it, and he's a-sitting in the very chair that Zeke was a-sitting in when he decided to go kill that man."

Wesley felt a thrill run through his body. He started thinking about Zeke Proctor and about Skylar.

They were both Cherokees. He thought about the decisive actions of Proctor and his own inclination to inaction. Perhaps this once in his life, he should act more like the Cherokees. Perhaps he should do something. His brother's very life was in danger. Perhaps he should find a way to break him out of jail and help him to escape into the wilds of the Cherokee Nation. He wondered if the current chief of the nation would help Skylar as Downing had helped Proctor. Perhaps.

Riding back home after darkness had fallen, each with a bit of a buzz from the whiskey, the brothers began discussing the upcoming trial of Skylar.

"Perhaps we should pay a visit to Judge Parker and see if we can't swing him over to Skylar's side," said Wesley.

"We could try that," said Keenan.

"And if that fails, we could smuggle a revolver in to Skylar."

"We could try that as well," said Keenan, "but that would be risky. First of all, the smuggling in of the gun would be far from certain, and even if we succeeded, Skylar would be in danger when he used it trying to escape."

"That's all true, but as a last resort, we should at least give it a try."

"Of course you're right. Let's start with the judge."

"Wait a minute, Brother," said Keenan with excitement in his voice, "when our father married Skylar's mother, did he not become a Cherokee citizen by marriage?"

"By heaven," said Wesley, "I believe you're right. Then the case should go to the Cherokee courts."

Freedom from a Soap Bubble

◆ ◆ ◆

Skylar made prayers to Unelanuhi. He did not know the proper forms, but he prayed anyway. He used what Cherokee words he knew, and the rest he said in English. He begged forgiveness for that, but said that he did not know any better. His mother had died when he was very young, and he had been raised by English-speaking people. He thought that Unelanuhi would understand.

He prayed for help in his coming trial, and he prayed that Bear's Mouth had known about this trouble when he made his medicine to help Skylar. He prayed that the medicine would be powerful enough to get him out of this mess. Even as he prayed for this help, he thought that he most likely deserved to be hanged. His whole life he had been a profligate, a wastrel. He had whored, and he had been a drunkard, and he had killed men. He had also threatened the life of his father and he had longed for his death. He had rejoiced in the news of the old man's death.

His only regret would be the loss of his love, the great love of his life, Adaline. She had at long last agreed to marry him, and he wanted that more than anything else in life. Now that could be taken from him. It hurt him deeply to think of losing that. And it was all the fault of old Phillip Garret, his father, the evil old reprobate. He wondered who the real killer was. He would like to congratulate him, to thank him for ridding the world of such a scoundrel.

"Garret."

The voice startled Skylar. He looked up to see a guard outside the cell. The man held something in his hand the shape of a brick. It was not quite so large though, and it was wrapped in brown paper. He held it through the bars. Skylar gave him a puzzled look.

"Here," the guard said. "This was left for you by an old Indian man with a gray beard."

Skylar walked over to the bars and took the package. The guard walked away. Skylar sat down on the edge of his bunk and looked at the strange package. *Bear's Mouth,* he said to himself.

Finally, he started to unwrap it. He threw the paper down on the floor. He was staring at what appeared to be a bar of soap. He rubbed it. He sniffed it. Lye soap, he thought.

He had a bucket of water in the cell, and he rolled up his sleeves and dipped the lye soap into the bucket and began washing his hands. The water was soon full of thick suds. He scrubbed some more, and bubbles began to rise up from the bucket and float around the cell. He looked at the suds astonished. Some began to float out through the bars on the cell window and on outside. He looked at them more closely, and he could see tiny men, one in each bubble. He thought they all looked very much like him. They went out and out.

Keenan and Wesley sat at the table in the Garret house. They had a bottle of brandy sitting on the table between them. Keenan picked up the bottle and poured their glasses full. He picked up his own glass and offered it to Wesley for a toast. Wesley clicked it with his glass.

"To the Garrets," said Keenan. "May they all live forever."

"All that are left," said Wesley.

They drank, and just then the front door burst open, and Skylar came running into the room.

"Skylar," said Wesley.

"How the hell did you get out of jail?" said Keenan.

"With a bar of soap," said Skylar.

Wesley got up and went into the kitchen. He returned with another glass, and Keenan poured it full of brandy. Wesley put it on the table in front of Skylar.

"But why are you here?" said Keenan. "They'll surely come here looking for you."

"Surely you are correct," Skylar said. "But they won't find me. I had to get out. I mean to wed."

"Skylar," said Wesley, "with all the evidence against you, this will just make it worse. If they catch you again, they'll surely hang you now."

"They might," said Skylar, "but don't be so sure of that."

"Brother," said Wesley, "what did you mean by the bar of soap?"

"Nothing. A joke."

"You must have meant something."

"Of course, but you wouldn't believe it."

"Tell us," said Keenan. "I'm sure we've believed stranger things."

"Well, then, someone sent me a bar of lye soap. I washed my hands with it, and bubbles began floating out the window. I left the cell in one of those bubbles."

"Oh, come on," said Wesley.

"I went to a Cherokee medicine man a while back," Skylar said. "He must have sent the soap. Do you believe that a burning bush spoke to Moses? Or that Jesus fed multitudes with a fish and loaf of bread? Or that he walked on water?"

"I, uh—

"Forget all that. I believe it," said Keenan. "Stinker made an astonishing discovery in our father's room."

"What was it?"

"He found papers that prove all of your claims. The house and all of the money belongs to you. We can prove it now."

"If it will do me any good. But that's wonderful. Where are these papers? Give them to me."

"I will get you the papers if you will get out of Arkansas and go back to the Cherokee Nation," said Keenan.

"Back to Webber's Falls? That's where they arrested me in the first place."

"Then somewhere else. Just get away from here."

"I will if you will do something for me. Go to Parker. Find out the date for the trial and tell him that I will be there."

"But why? If you can escape?"

"If I can't claim my inheritance, and if I can't live in peace and comfort with my wife-to-be, then I will not have escaped. Do this for me. Please, Brother."

"All right. I'll do it."

When the brothers split up to go their separate ways, Keenan went immediately to gather up the papers that Skylar was in need of. He wrapped them up carefully in an oilskin. He was terribly anxious to see Skylar again and deliver the papers to him. He made a trip to the courthouse the next morning to inquire about the date of the trial. The clerk of whom he was asking questions said, "But Skylar Garret has escaped from prison. The trial has been postponed indefinitely."

"But I have seen Skylar," said Keenan. "He has assured me that he will be at the trial if he can know the date."

"You know where he is?" said the clerk. "Come with me to see the marshal."

"I have nothing to tell the marshal," said Keenan. "I know nothing of Skylar's whereabouts."

"How are you to give him the information about the trial then?"

"He'll contact me. That's all."

"Come with me," said the clerk.

He led Keenan down the hall to an office where he knocked on the door lightly. A voice came from inside the office. "Who is it?"

It was a low and pleasant voice. The clerk answered. "It's Jarvis, sir. May I come in?"

"Certainly. Come in."

Jarvis opened the door a crack and slipped in, leaving Keenan standing in the hallway. "What is it?" said the marshal.

"I have Mr. Keenan Garret outside, sir. I believe he knows something about the whereabouts of Skylar Garret."

"Bring him in at once," said the marshal.

Jarvis opened the door wider. "Come in, Mr. Garret."

Keenan stepped in immediately and walked up to the desk. The man behind the desk was huge. Not portly but thickset. He appeared to be a powerful man with a slightly red face. Brown hair going just a bit bald on top. "I'm Keenan Garret," Keenan said. "I'm Skylar's brother."

"And you know where he is?"

"No, sir, I do not."

"But Jarvis said —

"Jarvis doesn't listen well," said Keenan. "I saw my brother yesterday. He asked me to tell the judge that he would be at the trial if he knew the date. Then he left. I have no idea where he went. I suspect he'll contact me to find out the date."

"Give me until this time tomorrow," said the marshal. "I'll have the date for you."

Skylar had gone from his house (he was calling it that now) to the home of his Adaline, and she had welcomed him in. They had immediately embraced and soon thereafter gone to bed to make passionate love throughout the night. When morning came they had not slept much. Even so, they arose and prepared breakfast and ate it together. After that they sat holding hands and drinking coffee. In Skylar's mind the only way he could find more happiness than he had at that moment would be to actually wed this vision of loveliness he knew as Adaline.

He put an arm around her shoulders and pulled her to him, and he kissed her tenderly and passionately. "I love you, my darling," he said. "I love you with all my life."

Skylar had accomplished much in a short while. He had gotten himself loose from Katherine at last. She had her money, and he had his freedom. Katherine was now married to his brother Keenan, and Skylar could not have been more content with that arrangement. His father was now dead, and he was clearly the owner of all of the property that he had been declaring was his by right. Keenan said he had the papers. And most important of all, he had Adaline's promise to marry him. He had completely and fully abandoned the Christian religion in favor of his own traditional religion. He now prayed to Cherokee gods and went for help to a Cherokee medicine man. His life was almost complete.

Skylar decided that Keenan had enough time. He went the next day to his house to look for him. He found his other brothers, Wesley and the Stinker, sitting at the big table drinking brandy. "Where is Keenan?" he demanded without even a greeting.

"He hasn't been here in two days," said Wesley.

"Sit down and have a drink, brother Garret," said the Stinker.

"I have to find Keenan," said Skylar.

"I should look at Katherine's house," said Wesley. "He is her husband, you know."

Skylar turned and ran out of the house. He jumped into the saddle and lashed his big stallion, racing back out the driveway toward the road. In three quarters of an hour, he found himself in front of Katherine's fine house. He dismounted before the horse had even stopped running, tied it to the fence and ran up to the front door. Even in his agitated state, he had the presence of mind to stop and rap on the door with the brass knocker. The door was opened by the servant girl. "Mr. Skylar," she said, surprised.

"Where is my brother?"

"Sit down, Mr. Skylar. I'll tell Mr. Keenan you're here."

"Well, hurry it up then," he said. He did not sit down though. He paced the floor, back and forth across the room. In a couple of minutes, Keenan appeared. He was carrying the oil cloth. "Skylar," he said, holding the packet out toward his brother. Skylar grabbed it greedily. "My papers?" he said.

"Yes," answered Keenan.

Skylar quickly unwrapped the bundle and laid out the papers on a table. He looked through them quickly. Finding everything in them he wanted, he folded them back and wrapped them again in the oilskin. He looked up anxiously at Keenan. "The trial date?" he asked.

When Skylar was completely satisfied, he left Katherine's house and mounted his horse. He turned the steed to head for the Cherokee Nation. Keenan was standing in the doorway on the porch. "I'll be at the trial," Skylar shouted. As he did, he noticed two men on horseback start to move toward him. Though they wore no uniforms, and he could see no badges, he thought the men had the look of United States marshals. He urged his horse to move a little faster. Looking over his shoulder, he saw that the two riders had also picked up their pace.

He continued to ride at that pace until he had reached the edge of town. Then he began to race. He looked back to see the two men racing their horses after him. They were U.S. lawmen. He knew that now. He considered pulling out one of his pistols and shooting them, but he quickly told himself that his action would just be added to the crimes with which they would charge him at the trial. He was so close now to all that he wanted, he did not want to do anything more to spoil his possibilities of success.

"I'll be at the trial."

♦ ♦ ♦

Why couldn't they leave him alone? He had said that he would be there for the trial. Why must they try to keep him locked up in that stinking cell between now and then? Did they not believe in honor? He would be there if they should decide to hang him. And if that should happen then this would decidedly be his last burst of freedom. *Leave me alone, you bastards.*

When Skylar crossed into the Cherokee Nation he looked behind himself. The marshals were still following him. They apparently decided that they had followed far enough, for all of a sudden they started shooting at him. Their shots were wild and wide, but he could hear the bullets whiz past him, and that made him a bit nervous. He rode harder. He looked for places to turn off, but the road was lined with thick brush. There was no safe place to get off the road. At long last, only a few miles from the turnoff to Webber's Falls, he saw a narrow lane turning off to his left. He glanced back and could not see the marshals. Chances were pretty good that they could not

191

see him either, so he turned quickly, so quickly that his horse came near falling over. He kept his feet though and continued racing down the narrow lane. Skylar found himself in a few miles on the banks of a river.

He slowed his mount to a comfortable walk, and in another moment rode into the deep woods. He dismounted and tied the horse to a small tree trunk. Then he walked back into the clearing. He looked down the lane in the direction from which he had come. There was no sign of pursuit. He figured that the marshals had figured he was going back into Webber's Falls to his old cabin. Well, he would fool them. He not only had not but he would not go back there again. There was nothing in the cabin that he needed or even wanted. He walked to the water's edge and got down to take a drink of the cool, clear, running water. It was good. He thought it was even better tasting than brandy or whiskey. There was a rock nearby, and he sat up and leaned back on it. He took out his pipe and tobacco and built himself a smoke.

The smoke was good, as he puffed out huge clouds of it and watched them rise up and slowly dissipate. He considered his predicament. There was at least a fair chance that he would be convicted and sentenced to hang. Judge Parker's reputation attested to that. But he was almost certain that his brothers and his cousin Mouse were working for him, trying to sway the judge or to hire him a good lawyer. And then there was the Indian medicine he had secured from Bear's Mouth. *Yes*, he told himself. He did have a chance of escaping this mess he had gotten himself into.

And once he was free, he told himself, *he would be in grand shape.* He had found out his Cherokee name, Noq'si. It meant Star. And he had a medicine man to go to with any problems. He was learning more and believing more in the old Cherokee religion. He had his Cherokee wife promised to him. He even had the papers proving his ownership of the Garret house in Fort Smith and of all the money that was left in his father's name. It was all his. He had every reason to expect a long and comfortable life ahead of him.

But there was one problem, and it had to do with that last, the house and the money. That was the white man in him, that desire for money and a big house. It was not a Cherokee thing, and it worried him that he wanted it. He should be content with the small cabin in Webber's Falls. Adaline should be content with it as well, but he was sure that she would not be. He would not be either. He wanted that big house, and he wanted the money. He had become too used to fine things in the white man's world. He could not get along without them at this point in his life. He had his fine guns, and he would keep them. He enjoyed good whiskey and good brandy. He liked dining in fine restaurants. He enjoyed going around in expensive clothing. Could he covet these things and still be a Cherokee? He did not know, and it worried him. He decided that he must pay another visit to old Bear's Mouth.

When he approached the cabin far in the woods, it was like the previous time. Bear's Mouth was standing on the porch leaning against a post and smoking. As Skylar drew nearer he could see that the old man had a smile on his face. He rode on up and dismounted, tying his horse to the post.

"'Siyo, Noq'si," said Bear's Mouth.

"'Siyo," said Skylar.

He stepped up onto the porch, and the two men sat on the chairs that were there. "How have you been?" Bear's Mouth asked.

"My health is fine," said Skylar. "There are other matters that brought me here."

"The killing of your father?"

"Yes. That. And more."

The medicine man mumbled and nodded his head. Skylar continued, and he told the whole story of the killing of old Phillip and everything that had happened since. He told of the upcoming trial and all of the evidence against him. He told about the two marshals who had followed him from Fort Smith. At long last he told about what had been bothering him the most. He confessed his desire for certain things of the white man, money and a fine house most of all.

Bear's Mouth puffed his pipe. He knocked the dottle out, and then he stood up. "Come with me," he said, and he led the way into his house. As Skylar stepped inside, Bear's Mouth gestured toward a far wall of the room. Skylar looked and saw hanging on the wall a rifle and a shotgun. "I keep those," said Bear's Mouth. "They come in handy. And my clothes are white man's clothes too. We can take from the white man what is useful to us. That's okay. Don't worry about it. I even pray to God in Jesus's name now and then. There's nothing wrong with that. It's all the same God. Different people call him by different names is all."

"So I can live in the Garret house?"

"It's yours. You can live in it."

"And the money? If I get rich?"

"That's just your good fortune." The old man sat down and motioned to another chair. Skylar sat in it. "Now about that other stuff. Keep on a-using that tobacco I made for you. It's for protection. It's all you need."

Skylar felt much better as he rode away from Bear's Mouth's house. But as he rode, doubts crept into his brain. Was the old man right? Were the Christians right? Who, in all the world, had the right answers? And how could he know? Suddenly he wanted to talk to his brother, Wesley. He did not know why he wanted to talk with Wesley. The questions in his mind were all to do with Cherokee stuff, Cherokee beliefs. What did Wesley know about that? Wesley and Keenan had come up with the notion about old Phillip having been a Cherokee citizen by marriage. That had been a good idea, and they had gone to the judge with it, but Parker had rejected the notion. He said that when Phillip had remarried to a white woman, he had forfeited that citizenship. Besides that, he was now an escapee, and he had to be brought to trial for that reason. The case, it seemed, had to go on in the federal court at Fort Smith. Still he had a powerful desire for answers to his big questions. He turned back toward Fort Smith.

When Skylar reached Fort Smith everything was dark. It was late into the night. As he rode up to the Garret house, it too was dark. He took his horse into the barn and unsaddled it. No one just riding by would see it. Then he went into the house. The doors were not locked. He found his way to the dining table where they all sat around drinking brandy. He went into the kitchen and fixed a pot of coffee. He smoked his pipe while waiting for the coffee to boil.

As he poured the last of the coffee into his cup, the Stinker came in. "Good morning, Brother," said Skylar. "I'm afraid that I've just poured the last of the coffee into my cup."

"I'll make some more," Stinker said. He went into the kitchen.

"Is Wesley here?" Skylar called out.

"He was here last night," said Stinker. "I believe he stayed the night here. Keenan too."

"Were you all up late drinking?"

"Yes. They may sleep until noon."

"Lazy bastards," said Skylar. "Why isn't Keenan at home with his wife?"

"I wondered about that myself," said Stinker. "I even asked him."

"And what did he answer?"

"He said, 'mind your business,' is all."

As the coffee boiled up and the Stinker poured himself a cup and then refilled Skylar's cup, Wesley came walking in.

"Ah, Wesley," said Skylar, "it's you I came to see. Good morning, Brother."

"What the hell are you doing here, Skylar, or Star," said Wesley. "The lawmen are looking all over for you."

"They won't find me here," Skylar said. "Sit down and have some coffee. I want to talk to you."

Stinker poured Wesley a cup, and Wesley sat down. "What is it that's so important?" he said.

"I've been to see my medicine man again," Skylar said. "You know, way back before the Removal, they say an old Cherokee prophet came down out of the mountains and told the people to get rid of everything they had from the white man. He even told them to kill all their cats. If they failed in this, he said, they would be driven west. They didn't heed him, and here we are. You know, I have been attempting to live a more Cherokee life. I've been worrying about this my fine house, my fine clothes, my guns, my money and all that. I asked my medicine man about it, and he said it was all right. He said take what you can use from the white man. It's okay. I want to know what you think about that."

"I don't know, brother," said Wesley. "Both arguments seem sound to me. It seems that if you want to hold on to your old identity, then you should not bother with things from another culture. On the other hand, it doesn't seem so bad to live in a fine house, if you continue to believe in the old things from your culture. It seems to me that what you believe is what's important, and it would be particularly important if you had children. You would want to bring your children up properly, I would think."

"So you would not disagree with the medicine man?"

"No. I think I would not."

197

"There is another matter, perhaps more important. He also told me that it is not important what we call God when we pray to him, because he said there is but one God, though different peoples call him by different names. What do you in all your godliness think about that?"

"I don't think it matters a jot, because I don't believe he hears you. I don't think he exists at all, so what the hell do you care?"

"You've been infected by our atheist brother Keenan," said Skylar. "How did that happen? You were the good one. I had trust in you, Wesley. What would your holy preacher think of what has become of you?"

"I can't help it," said Wesley. "There are too many bad things happening on this earth. I can no longer believe in him."

"But God gave us free will, did he not? Isn't that the standard explanation for all of those things? God created us and then let us loose to do good or bad. He doesn't interfere with our behavior."

"That's what they say."

"Why can you not accept it that way then?"

"I just can't," said Wesley. "It's unfathomable."

"If God is all powerful and all good, how can he just watch and not interfere? Remember when you came across the boys beating up the Indian boy? Why did you not behave like God and just watch them?"

"I was able to help, and I saw a need. I—

"Can not God see the same things? Why does he just watch and let bad things happen?"

"I don't know. Reverend Wright couldn't even answer that question for me. What would your medicine man say?"

"I don't know, Wesley. This is all beyond my powers of thought. This is why I came to you, but you're not being any help to me. None at all."

"I'm sorry, but I can't help it. You just have to work it all out for yourself. Believe or don't believe. I have worked it out for myself, and I don't believe."

"But I must. I must believe."

"Then you will."

Wesley sipped his coffee, and then he said, "I have a question for you, Skylar. Your trial is scheduled right away. I believe it's the day after tomorrow. Are you going to be there, or will you run away?"

"I'll be there if I live. I've said I'll be there, haven't I?"

The Devil's Visit

◆ ◆ ◆

Keenan was not down for coffee for a very good reason. He was sleeping hard and late, but restlessly. He did not know actually if he was asleep or awake. He felt like he was awake and trying desperately to go to sleep. He sat up and looked across the room, and he saw sitting there on the far end of the couch a well dressed young gentleman, looking at him and smiling. "What the Devil?" Keenan shouted. "How did you get in here?" He got up and rushed to the door. It was still locked, as he knew he had left it. He ran to the window and found it locked as well. Then, "I've seen you before," he said. "Where was it? When?"

"We had a visit not long ago," said the peculiar gentleman, "right here in this room."

"But I'm dreaming," said Keenan, "and you're not real."

"I feel real, as real as you."

"Then I can kill you."

"Perhaps you can."

"I don't have a gun, but I can bash out your brains with a candlestick or something."

"I don't think it will do you any good," said the stranger. "In fact, I don't believe you can really kill me."

"What makes you think that?"

"Because I am you. I was created out of your brain. Go ahead. Try to kill me."

"You do resemble me somewhat," said Keenan.

"I am you. But then, I may be someone else, too."

"You talk like a fool. How can you be me and someone else at the same time?"

"It's not difficult. And it's all out of your peculiar brain."

"You are a fool."

"Why do you keep insulting me? I've done you no harm."

"Tell me why you're here."

"I'm here because something is bothering you, and you wanted someone to talk with about it."

"I don't know what you're talking about. My father was recently murdered right here in this house, and my brother is going on trial in the morning accused of the murder and theft of three thousand dollars. I'm afraid he might be convicted, and I know that he's innocent, but I don't want to talk about that with you."

"Of course you do. Your brother who is going on trial is called Skylar."

"How do you know that?"

"I told you, I am you. But the murder was actually committed by your other brother. The one who is called the Stinker."

"Damn you. You can't know these things."

"My other identity is known by many names."

"The Devil you say."

"I didn't say it. You did."

"You're the Devil?"

"I'm the Devil if you say I am."

"I don't believe in you, not you and not God."

"But you must believe in me for I came out of your brain."

"You're a fool."

"I recall a paper you wrote some years ago in which you said that since there is no God, man may make of himself a god, and then he may make his own rules, his own laws, if you will, and then he will stand alone in the highest place and be adored. I am standing in that high place, and I was created out of your brain."

Keenan leaped up from where he sat and grabbed a brandy glass from off the table. He flung it with all his might at the spectre, screaming, "Get out. Get out of here. You're a fool and a liar. Go away."

The spectre vanished, and as he did, Keenan could still hear his voice trailing off. "Ah, he remembers Luther, but he could not locate an inkwell to throw at me. I am you. I am you. I am you."

Keenan covered his eyes with his hands and squinted hard. In a moment he opened them again, and the Devil was there again with a ghastly look on his face. He was staring at Keenan wide eyed. Keenan ran toward him. Rather he walked, but he thought he was running. His steps were long strides, but they were slow, and there was a pause after each one. His arms were flailing, as though he were swimming through water. The Devil retreated from him, still staring at him in horror. He was walking backward, not running. It was a strange chase, with both parties moving slowly but desperately. Then the Devil was backing up a stairway with a stone wall to his right. When Keenan reached the stairway he started up after the Devil. Both continued as before. At last the Devil reached a landing of sorts, and he backed to the edge and stopped, looking over his shoulder at a tremendous drop to the earth. He held his hands in front of his face in a protective mode. Keenan made the last three long steps until he came close, and then he reached out with both hands and clutched the lapels of the Devil's jacket. He noticed that the jacket was exactly like his own. He pulled the Devil toward him and then shook him violently. Finally he turned loose with his right hand and drew it back. He made a fist and smashed it into the Devil's jaw. He felt bones crunch. He heard a scream, and he stepped back. The Devil flew backward into space, while Keenan stood there dumbfounded, staring over the precipice into the darkness out there.

"It was the Devil," he said. "By God, it was the Devil."

And then he found himself sitting up in his bed staring into the darkness of his empty bedroom.

Keenan went to the table against the wall where a bowl and a pitcher of water sat. He grabbed up the pitcher and poured water into the bowl, and then he splashed his face liberally with it. He picked up a towel and dried his face, then he hurriedly dressed himself and went downstairs. He found Skylar and Wesley drinking coffee. Wesley got up and poured Keenan a cup of coffee. Keenan looked absolutely frantic. "What's the matter, brother?" said Wesley. "Sit down and drink some coffee. It will be good for you. Sit down." He pulled out a chair for Keenan. Keenan sat down heavily. He picked up the cup and sipped the hot liquid.

"I've had a visitor," he said.

"A visitor?" said Skylar. "But no one has come into the house."

"This one did," said Keenan. "He got into my room, though the door and the window were both locked."

"How could that be?" asked Wesley.

"It was the Devil. He said he was the Devil, and he said he was me. He came out of my brain, he said."

"So it was nothing but a dream," said Skylar.

"It was real. He was as real as you are. I threw a glass at him, and he left the room."

"There is no Devil," said Wesley.

"But there is. I've been visiting with him. And I—I killed him."

"I have denounced him along with God. He does not exist. You've been dreaming."

"But he was here—in my room—and he was tormenting me. He talked about our father's murder. He said—"

"Did he accuse me?" said Skylar.

"No. He knew that you are innocent."

"Then who?"

"He accused—the Stinker."

"Isn't it ironic, Brothers, that our atheist brother, Keenan, the intellectual has just talked with the Devil. Of course, I have always heard it said that an atheist doesn't believe in God. I've never heard whether or not he believes in the Devil."

"God damn you all," shouted Keenan. "I fought with him. I threw him over a wall, a wall of a high precipice, and he plunged down to his death."

"Good," said Wesley, "then there is no more Devil. We should all be the better for it."

The Trial Begins

♦ ♦ ♦

When Skylar appeared at the court house on the appointed day and at the appointed time, he was immediately approached by two deputy marshals, one of whom grabbed each arm and escorted him inside.

"There's no need for this," said Skylar. "I'm here just as I said I would be."

"We want to make sure you stay," said one of the deputies.

They marched him to a table near the front of the court room and sat him down. Then they sat on each side of him. Both deputies were armed with side arms. Skylar thought how easy it would be to take one of the guns from one of the deputies and shoot his way out of the court room. He smirked at the thought. Wesley came into the room with another man and brought the man to Skylar's table. "Skylar," he said, "I've brought you an attorney. This is Mr. J. Warren Reed. Mr. Reed, this is my brother, Skylar Garrett."

"This is the defendant?" asked Reed.

"Yes sir."

Reed shook hands with Skylar. "Your brother has filled me in on the case, Mr. Garrett. Don't worry. We'll beat them," he said.

"Thank you, Mr. Reed ," said Skylar. "I am innocent of these charges. But I can't pay you."

"Don't concern yourself with that. My fee has been taken care of—by Mr. Mouse."

Just then Judge Parker walked in the room, and the entire courtroom was called to their feet. The judge sat down, and everyone else was seated again. The judge called the case, rapped with his gavel and declared court to be in session. He read the charges against Skylar and had Skylar stand up. "How do you plead to these charges?" he demanded.

Skylar stood up to his tallest. He was dressed in a fine suit and carrying a walking stick. "Your Honor," he said, in a loud and clear voice, "I am guilty of being a drunk, a womanizer and a general scoundrel, but I am innocent of the charges you read against me. I am innocent of the blood of my father."

"Mr. Garrett," said the judge, "from here on you will confine yourself to answering only the question which is asked of you."

"Yes, your Honor," said Skylar. "I beg your Honor's pardon."

The prosecutor, William H. H. Clayton, called his first witness. It was Mr. Gray Mouse, and he asked Mouse about the evening he had spent in the mission with the Garrets and Reverend Wright. Mouse admitted that Skylar was somewhat vindictive regarding the money he claimed had been left him by his mother that he had never received. He claimed that Phillip, his father, had kept it for himself. When Reed cross-examined, Mouse said that Phillip had been a sorry father indeed to Skylar, and that he personally believed Skylar's claims about the money. He said that Phillip had not even raised Skylar, his own son, but had left the raising of him to his servant, the former slave, old Jacob. Under cross-examination, Mouse had proved to be a better witness for the defense than for the prosecution.

Skylar's brother Keenan was called, and he told the court that Phillip and Skylar had both been in love with the same woman, the Cherokee woman Adaline. He said that he had been ashamed of his father for courting a woman so much younger than himself. When he was pressed by Clayton, he admitted that Skylar had been engaged to marry another woman, a white woman by the name of Katherine Durwood. And he owed Miss Durwood a thousand dollars. He needed the money so he could pay her back, and once he had done that, he would ask her to release him from his promise of marriage. Then he would be free to ask Miss Adaline for her hand.

Adaline and Katherine Durwood were both seated in the crowd watching and listening to the proceedings with rapt attention. When Katherine was referred to in the witnesses' remarks, she would blush slightly and put her fan in front of her face. Anytime Adaline was mentioned, she would sit up straighter and develop a slight smirk on her face.

"Mr. Garrett," said Clayton to Keenan, "did you ever hear your brother Skylar, the defendant here, threaten the life of your father, Mr. Phillip Garrett?"

There was a slight pause before Keenan answered, "Yes. On numerous occasions, but he..."

"Do you believe that your brother killed your father — his father?"

"If you mean my brother Skylar, no sir, I do not."

On cross-examination, Reed asked Keenan why he did not believe that Skylar had committed the murder. Keenan's answer astonished the entire courtroom. "Because," he said, "my other brother, the Stinker, told me, confessed to me that he had done the deed."

Judge Parker had to rap hard over and over with his gavel and shout out for order in the courtroom. At last everyone quieted down again and the trial proceeded. A few more witnesses were called, each of whom spoke of instances during which they had heard Skylar curse his father and even threaten to kill him. The court recessed for the day, and everyone left to go home.

The Stinker

♦ ♦ ♦

The Stinker was in his dirty little hovel next to the
Garrett house alone. He was drinking brandy he had
pilfered from the big house, and he was well nigh drunk.
He thought about his three legitimate brothers.
Particularly about his brother Skylar who was on trial for
murder and could well hang for it. He also thought about
his brother Keenan to whom he had confessed his crime.
What if Keenan told on him at the trial? Would they
come for him? Would they charge him with the crime,
put him on trial? Then it might well be he who would
hang and not Skylar.

He thought that he liked his three brothers. He liked
being the fourth Garrett brother. It would have been nice
though if he had some real name. Not just Stinker.
Stinker Garrett? What kind of name was that? He could
be a George or Herman even. But no. He was just the
Stinker. What kind of miserable life had his mother lived
here among these stuck-up people? He wondered if he

had any worthwhile time left to live in his life. He did not think so.

He thought, if he were to die there would be no evidence against him except the word of Keenan, and he did not think that would be enough to save Skylar. He asked himself if he really wanted Skylar to hang, and he could not answer the question. He decided that he did not care. Skylar's death would likely throw the entire Garrett family into a monstrous turmoil, and he was certain they deserved it. He walked, rather staggered across the room and picked up a coil of rope, and then as he staggered back, looking up at the ceiling for a spot where the great beam crossed over an open space on the floor, he kicked a stool along in front of him.

Once he kicked the stool completely over, and he had to bend over to pick it up again. But when he bent, he fell. "God damn it all the way down to hell," he said. He struggled back to his feet nearly falling again. Then he looked up. A heavy duty steel hook had been driven into the beam some years ago. Stinker had no idea why. He had never made any use of it. He tied one end of the rope to the heavy dresser in his room, and he tugged at it then to make sure that the dresser would be heavy enough to hold. Then he tied a loop in the other end and put it over his head. He snugged the loop around his neck. Finally he stepped up onto the stool and reached up high with both hands to loop the rope over the hook. He shoved his hands down deep in his pockets and smirked.

"Fuck the Garretts," he shouted at the top of his lungs, and he kicked backwards with his feet toppling the stool. Suddenly he was dangling by the rope around his neck. He had a surprise thought. "I made a mistake. I shouldn't have done that." His feet kicked back and around wildly, searching for the stool, but they could not find it. As he spun around on the end of the rope, he saw the overturned stool some feet away. There was no way he could reach it. His hands went up to the rope around his neck and clutched it. He tried desperately to loosen the loop, but to no avail.

He gagged, he coughed, he spluttered and drooled. He gasped for breath. His legs continued kicking and flailing. He felt the cock in his pants stiffen. He felt his bowels loosen. At last he stopped kicking. He stopped gagging and gasping. His arms dropped to his sides, and he hung there spinning slowly around, alone and dead.

The next morning, Jacob had the buggy ready and waiting, and Keenan and Wesley came out of the house dressed in their best. They were ready to head for the courthouse. "Let's get going, Jacob," said Keenan.

"But where is Stinker?" Jacob said, looking around.

"Perhaps he decided not to go today," said Wesley.

"I think I better go check on him," said Jacob, and he went toward Stinker's shack.

Wesley looked at Keenan. "I hope he hurries," he said. "I don't want us to be late."

Jacob came running back in another moment. He had a ghastly expression on his face. "Boys," he said. "Come with me."

Neither Keenan nor Wesley questioned him. He looked absolutely terrified. They both jumped out of the buggy and followed him to the Stinker's room. When they went in they all stopped and stared at the horrible sight there in front of them. There was a fowl smell hanging in the air, and, of course, Stinker too was hanging there.

But Who Will Listen?

♦ ♦ ♦

When the brothers arrived at the courthouse the following morning, they noticed an old Cherokee man standing to the right side of the doorway leaning against the wall. He was heavy set and wore a gray beard. His head was bare, and he was slightly bald on top. He had a slight smile on his old face, and he nodded at the brothers as they passed into the building. They did not know him, but he had caught their attention.

Keenan got himself on the witness stand soon after the trial got going. He had briefed Reed on what he wanted to say. Reed asked a few preliminary questions before he got to the point. "You have another brother who is not here right now?"

"Yes."

"And what is his name?"

"He is known only as the Stinker. He was an illegitimate offspring of my father."

215

"The Stinker," said Reed. "And did you have a conversation with him recently that is relevant to this case?"

"I did."

"Will you tell the court about that conversation?"

"Yes sir, I will. I went to my father's room, and I found Stinker there. He had been going through father's papers, and he had found proof that father was holding Skylar's money. We looked further and found evidence that the house did indeed belong to Skylar as well. Then we began discussing this case, our brother Skylar's situation. I said that I did not believe Skylar had committed the crime, and Stinker said that he did not either. I asked him why he felt that way, and he said to me that he himself had done the deed."

"Stinker said that he was the real murderer?"

"That is correct, Mr. Reed."

"And did he supply you with any details?"

"He did."

"And will you now give those details to the court?"

"Yes sir. He said that he heard a commotion in our father's room, and he went to investigate. When he drew close to the room, he could hear voices, the voices of my father and of my brother Skylar. He waited outside the room. He heard a gunshot. It frightened him, and he backed away. A moment later, Skylar rushed from the room and out of the house. Stinker went into the room to check on our father. He found the old man standing there trembling. He ran past him to where he knew that our father kept a revolver, and he got the revolver. Then he bashed in the old man's head."

"And you believed his tale?"

"I did believe him."

"Why is that?"

"Stinker was my brother, my half brother actually, but our father never acknowledged him as a Garret. Instead he treated him like a servant, more like a slave. He hated father for that treatment, and he knew that father had three thousand dollars on him that night."

"What was the money for? Was Mr. Garret in the habit of keeping so much money with him?"

"He was not. He had sent a letter to Adaline asking her to come to his house that evening. He meant to give her the money to buy new clothes for their wedding."

"What became of the money?"

"Stinker had it, and he gave half of it to me, and asked me to share generously with him when I came into the money that our father left."

"And Stinker is not in the courtroom this morning?"

"No sir, he is not. He hanged himself last night."

"So he is dead, and we have only your word to rely on for his confession?"

"Unfortunately, sir, that is true."

Adaline was called next, and she was asked about the invitation to go to the Garret house on that fateful day. "I received such a letter," she said, "but I had no intention of going there."

"And what about the wedding?"

"There was to be no wedding. I would not have married that old drunken lecher."

"Were you planning to marry his son, Skylar?"

"I was and I am."

Other witnesses were called by the prosecution, Wesley, men who had been at the parties Skylar had attended, Katherine, various people from around Fort Smith. All of them testified that they had heard Skylar accuse his father of hoarding money that belonged to him, of living in a house that was rightfully his, and they had actually heard him say that he would kill his father to get what was his. Old Jacob was called, and he said that he had heard the gunshot on the night of the murder, had gotten out of bed and run toward the big house, but on rounding the corner of the house had run right into Skylar who was running away, and Skylar had bashed him on the head with the butt of his revolver.

The deputies were called who had arrested Skylar in Webber's Falls. They each testified to his arrogant attitude and to the fact that he had escaped from prison. They also said that they had arrested him for another killing entirely. Everything was stacked against Skylar except Keenan's claim that Stinker had confessed to him.

The examination and cross examination of the witnesses went on all day. The courtroom was crowded with the interested and the curious. Among them was old Bear's Mouth, watching and listening to the proceedings with great interest. Skylar in his place at the table was extremely nervous. He had heard his brother tell the tale of the confession and the suicide of Stinker with great interest. Perhaps, he thought, there was some hope for him after all, but the words of the lawyer rang in his ears. "So we have only your word. . ." Perhaps the jury would not believe Keenan's word. The time came for the prosecutor's summation to the jury.

"Gentlemen," he said, drawing himself up to his fullest height and hooking his thumbs under the lapels of his vest, "you have heard the testimony and the cross examinations of all the witnesses. I believe you have but one recourse—to find the defendant, Mr. Skylar Garret, guilty of the heinous crime of patricide. We have proved that Skylar Garret bashed his own father's brains out with the butt of his revolver. You have listened to one witness after another tell us of how the defendant made no secret of his jealousy, of his belief that he was entitled to the house and all the money that was in the possession of Phillip Garret, his father. He believed, or so he claimed, that it was all his by right. Further he maintained over and again and in front of numerous witnesses that he would get what was rightfully his if he had to kill his father to get it. To add to his motive for this awful murder, he and his father were pursuing the same woman, this Adaline, with the intention of making her his wife. That in itself is despicable. Skylar Garret is well known in our community as a wild young man, a drunkard, a gambler, a killer and a womanizer. Finally, we have the word of the old servant Jacob that after he heard the shot and went running to the main house, he ran into Skylar Garret running away from the house, and Skylar Garret struck him in the head with the butt of his revolver. The same way he had murdered his father. Old Jacob is lucky to be alive. I know that you will return the right verdict."

It was Mr. Reed's turn. He stood up solemnly and strode to the jury box. Without speaking, he looked at each individual juror, and then he started pacing back and forth in front of them. It was several minutes before he spoke. If his intention was to created tension, he certainly succeeded. Everyone in the courtroom was nervous. Mr. Clayton had just about convinced them all of Skylar's guilt. Even Skylar was thinking that the jury should pronounce him guilty, for he deserved to hang for the wretched life he had lived. When Reed at last spoke it was in a loud and booming voice that startled all of the people almost out of their seats.

"Gentlemen," he said, "you have heard a great deal of damning evidence against my client, damning but circumstantial. You have heard nothing that proves his guilt. The only thing that has been proven against him is the bonking on the head of old Jacob, and old Jacob has assumed that since my client bonked him on the head, he must have also bashed in Phillip Garret's head. Such is not necessarily true. Any one of us may bonk someone on the head at any time for any number of reasons, especially if we should run into him at night and be startled. So declare Skylar Garret guilty of hitting an old servant on top of the head if you must, but do not declare him guilty of murder.

"The bulk of the evidence you have heard today has to do with the number of times my client was heard to say that he would kill his father. How many of us have said the same or something of equally horrendous character simply because we were angry at something? And Skylar Garret was certainly angry. He was angry at his father for having disinherited him of his home and his fortune. That is no proof of the crime of murder. Have you ever in anger shouted out at someone, 'I will kill you'? Or have you cried out as someone just left the room, 'I'll kill him'? I'm sure you have. I know I have. But did we do it? No. We did not.

"How many of you knew old Phillip Garret? How many of you wished that he would die or just go away somewhere and leave our community? He was a reprobate and a scoundrel. He was well known in these parts and very much disliked. And it is well-known that he neglected his own sons and left them in the hands of old Jacob to raise, and then had them sent away to school, all of them except the Stinker who he always denied and kept around only as a servant. He was a sorry excuse for a father and a sorry excuse for a man. If any man ever deserved to be killed, he did. He was the one.

"But we do not have to make excuses for his murder in order to free my client. All we need to do is to cast a doubt on his guilt, and we have done so. First there is no direct evidence of his guilt. None. Everything is circumstantial. No one witnessed the murder. Second there is the evidence given by his brother Keenan Garret that the Stinker confessed to him that he, the Stinker, had actually done the killing. And to back up Keenan Garret's story, we know that the Stinker had been treated very badly by Phillip Garret, who in fact was his father as well. And Stinker knew that old Garret had three thousand dollars on him.

"Gentlemen, you cannot send a man to his death on circumstantial evidence. You cannot condemn a man to death when there is another possibility. Skylar Garret is not the only one who could have done this deed. There is another. There is the Stinker. You cannot send a man to the gallows on the basis of loose talk. 'I will kill him. I will kill you.' You cannot and you will not do that. You must find Skylar Garret innocent of these charges."

Skylar, having been convinced by the words of Clayton that he must hang, was now swayed by Reed's eloquence that he was absolutely innocent and must be freed. He was reminded of the crowd in Julius Caesar who was convinced by Brutus that Caesar's death was necessary and then by Mark Antony that they should kill Brutus. He wondered about the jury. He wondered about the crowd. He turned in his chair to look over the crowd, and he saw sitting there in the midst of them old Bear's Mouth. Bear's Mouth saw him and caught him with his eyes. He smiled. Skylar turned back in his seat to face the front of the courtroom. He saw Judge Parker sitting there with a stern look on his face. He is hoping for a guilty verdict, Skylar thought, so he can sentence me to hang.

The jury was sent out to the jury room to deliberate. Skylar was taken back to his cell to await the verdict. The judge went to his chambers. Keenan Garret went to the side of his recent bride and whispered in her ear. She got up and walked to the judge's chambers. There was a deputy standing guard there. She spoke to him, introducing herself and saying that she wished to speak with the judge. The deputy knocked on the door and went inside. He came back and said that she might go in. He held the door for her and she walked boldly into Judge Parker's chambers. The judge stood up behind his desk and held out a hand.

"Katherine," he said, "how good to see you. What can I do for you?"

"Judge," she said, "you know that I was once engaged to be married to Skylar Garret."

"Of course," he said. "I believe just about everyone in Fort Smith knows that."

"Even though our engagement was called off and I married his brother Keenan, I do not believe that Skylar is guilty. I want you to know that he could not have done this deed. He is a good man, Judge. I know him, and I believe in him. If the jury should find him guilty, Judge, I hope you can find it in your heart to be lenient. I pray that you will."

"Katherine," said Parker, "I have all kinds of faith in your feelings."

The Verdict

◆ ◆ ◆

A huge crowd was gathered outside the courtroom, and they were all talking to one another about the trial. "Kill his father?" said one. "Why, I could never think of killing my own father."

"It's a terrible thing."

"But maybe he didn't do it."

"Who then?"

"There's that other one. The one who hanged himself."

"The Stinker."

"Yes. That one. Did you ever see him?"

"I saw him once. He looked like a killer for sure."

"But no one saw him do it."

"No one saw the other one do it either."

"No one saw the murder."

"Say, that Adaline's a good looker."

"Katherine Durwood's not bad either."

"You mean Garret. Katherine Garret.. She married one of them, you know."

"Yes. She married Keenan."

"But Skylar could have had both of those women."

"Maybe he did."

"That's no way to talk."

"Some men have all the luck."

"He'll hang though."

"No, he won't. He'll get off."

"Did you look at the jury? They all had mean looks on their faces. They'll find him guilty, for sure."

"Twenty dollars says you're wrong."

"You want to know what I think? I think that it's God's business to punish the guilty. They should turn Skylar loose and leave it all in God's hands."

"God has already done it. He made the killer hang himself."

"You mean the Stinker?"

"Sure. That's it."

At five o'clock someone came out the door to disperse the crowd. "Court has been recessed," he said. "Come back in the morning at ten o'clock."

In the jury room someone was saying, "I think the Stinker did it. I think he was telling the truth when he told Keenan that he had done it."

"But we don't know that he even said that. We only have Keenan's word for it."

"Keenan Garret is a philosopher, a published author. He's honest."

"A published author and a philosopher can lie as well as anyone else."

"I suppose so, but still I believe Keenan."

"Why would Skylar kill his old man when he had the proof about his property? He had no reason anymore."

"That's true."

"Did Skylar know about the papers before the murder?"

"I think we have to go on that thing they say about 'the shadow of a doubt.'"

Keenan and Wesley went to the jail and asked to be let in to see Skylar. He was surprised to see them. Jumping up from his cot, he smiled and reached for their hands. "Brothers," he said, "what a surprise. I had begun to think that I was alone in this world. A sorry and lost reprobate waiting to be condemned."

"You are no such thing, Skylar," said Wesley. "The verdict is not yet in, and you may be freed."

"You are certainly not alone," said Keenan. "We know you are innocent. There is no doubt at all in my mind."

"It's not your mind that worries me, Brother," said Skylar. "It's the minds of the judge and the jury."

"Mr. Reed was very convincing," Keenan said.

"Yes indeed," said Wesley.

"Yes," said Skylar. "I have to rely on what Reed said to the jury. He's my only hope at this point. Until he spoke his summation, I had given up all hope."

"Never give up hope," Keenan said. "You have been to your medicine man?"

"Yes. Of course, and he was in the courtroom today."

"Was he indeed?" said Wesley.

"Yes. You must have seen him. A somewhat portly man with a gray beard and a bald head."

"I think I saw him," Keenan said. "Standing outside the courtroom and smoking."

"Yes," said Wesley, "I saw him inside too, a Cherokee man with a keen interest in the case."

"And I still have his medicine. It will save me. It must."

At that moment, Adaline was let into the cell. She and Skylar embraced. "Oh, Skylar," she said, "the jury must find you innocent."

Skylar's confidence suddenly improved. "They will," he said. "Of course, they will. My brother Keenan gave them the truth of what happened, and I have the medicine that Bear's Mouth gave me. I'm certain to win this case."

"Oh, I'm sure they will. They must. We have so much to live for."

"And we will, my love. We will. You know, I got out of here before, and I can do it again, if need be. We'll be together—somewhere. I hope it's here in my house. We've proved now that I own the house and all the money. We could live very well. Very well indeed."

"You have to survive the jury first," said Keenan.

"Keenan," said Wesley, "I think we should leave them alone. Don't you?"

"Yes. I'm sure that you're right."

Skylar quickly grabbed both of their hands. "Brothers, thank you so much for coming to see me. It means a great deal to me to know that you're with me at this time. I love you both."

"Skylar," said Wesley, "know that I love you too."

"And I as well," said Keenan. "I love you, Brother."

The two Garret brothers left the cell, leaving Sylar and Adaline alone together. They embraced and they kissed as if it would be the last time. In another few minutes, the guards came to get Skylar. "The jury is in," they said.

Back in the courtroom, Skylar was again seated between two deputy marshals. Mr. Reed was seated at the same table. The judge asked the foreman of the jury if the jury had reached a verdict.

"We have, Your Honor," said the foreman.

The judge ordered the verdict to be read. Skylar was told to stand. The foreman handed the verdict to a deputy who carried it to the clerk. The clerk unfolded the paper and looked at it. The suspense was almost too much for Skylar to bear. He felt his knees growing weak, and he was trembling. Perspiration popped out on his forehead.

"We find the defendant—NOT GUILTY."

Skylar very near fainted. He was held up by the two deputies. The judge dismissed the case. Wesley, Keenan and Adaline rushed to Skylar's side, and all tried to embrace him at once.

"It's all over," said Keenan.

"You're free," said Wesley.

"Please take me home," Skylar said.

Life Goes On

♦ ♦ ♦

Keenan, Wesley and Adaline went to the Garret house with Skylar. They sat around the table and had a drink together. After one celebratory drink, however, Skylar declared that he'd had enough. He was tired and wanted to go to bed. Keenan excused himself and left to go home to his wife. Wesley also left, though he did not say where he was going. Outside the house, Wesley and Keenan said farewell to one another. Mounted up, they rode off in different directions. Wesley headed for the mission.

When he reached the mission, he dismounted and tied his horse to the rail in front of the main building. He walked in. No one was around. He was glad of that. He went to Reverend Wright's old room and stepped inside. It was still as the reverend had left it. Wesley knelt down beside the bed where the great man had slept. He began weeping.

"Lord God," he said, "I have strayed. I have been a sinner. I fell into the belief that all men are sinners, or that at the least all of my family were sinners. Since I am a Garret, I believed that I too was wicked, and so I drank and I cursed. But now you have showed me that things can be good. They can work out for the best. My brother Keenan has gone home to his wife, as he should, but most of all, the court has said that my brother Skylar is not guilty of the murder of our father. And now he will marry and live the life of a good husband to his wife. Bless them all, Father. Let their lives be good. And receive me back into the fold. I repent of my sins. I love you, Lord. All things work out as you will them to. Let me resume my studies so that I may become a preacher. I would like to take up the work of Reverend Wright. Thank you, Lord. I pray to you in the name Jesus Christ, our Savior. Amen."

Keenan showed up at the Garret house in a carriage with his wife. The two of them were let in by Jacob, who called Skylar. Skylar appeared with his intended Adaline, and the four of them sat down at the dining table. Jacob poured brandy all around.

"Well, Brother," said Keenan, "how does it feel to be entertaining guests in your house?"

"It feels right, Keenan. I've known all along this was my house, but it took your help to prove it. I'm glad that you and your lovely Katherine are my first house guests."

"And we are delighted that Adaline is here with you to receive us," said Katherine.

"Our younger brother, I believe, has returned to the mission," said Skylar.

"Yes," said Keenan, "and I believe he intends to return to school and prepare himself to take the place of the late Reverend Wright."

"He will be happy, I believe. He has found his way for sure. He lost it only for a short while."

"Yes, and I too have learned something through our—your—ordeal. I have discovered that there is indeed a God. I had to learn it from the Devil. So how are you, Brother?"

And Skylar, who was happiest of all the brothers, said, "I too have found my God, by a different name."

"So," said Keenan, "we three Garret brothers are all happy at last."

"Yes," said Skylar, "but is our fourth brother the Stinker happy in that place where his soul has landed?"

"And our father, I wonder," said Keenan.

Coming Soon!

AWARD-WINNING AUTHOR
MARDI OAKLEY MEDAWAR

For more information
visit: www.SpeakingVolumes.us

On Sale Now!

SHERIFF LANSING MYSTERIES
Books 1 – 6

For more information
visit: www.SpeakingVolumes.us

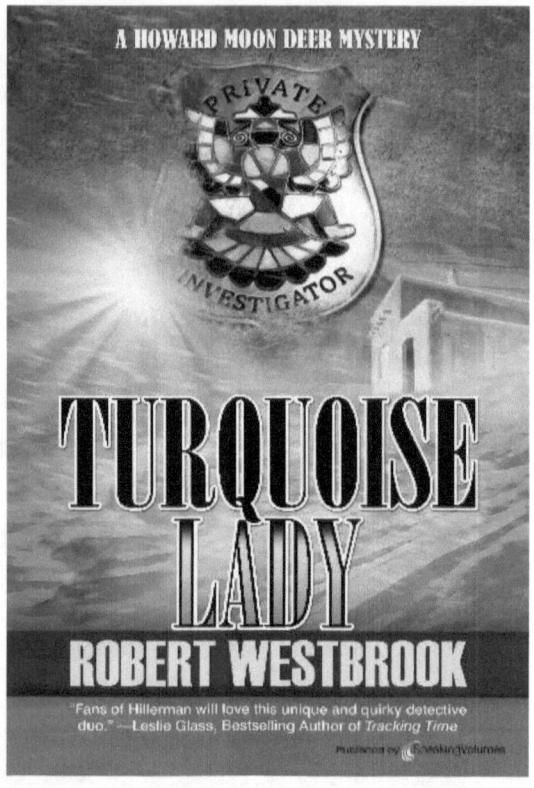

On Sale Now!

HOWARD MOON DEER MYSTERIES
Books 1 – 4

"Terrific…I couldn't put it down."
—Margaret Truman, author of *Murder at the Watergate*

On Sale Now!

STAR SONG *series*
Books 1 – 3

"If you're hungry for a book to keep you up past bedtime—with all the lights on—this tale is for you. Based on real unsolved mysteries, *Evil Chasing Way* deals with startling animal deaths that some attribute to aliens, skinwalkers, secret government research or a force of true evil. This is New Mexico's own X File anchored in Hausman's elegant prose and finely tuned descriptions of the Southwestern landscape."
—Anne Hillerman, author of *Song of the Lion*

EVIL CHASING WAY

GERALD HAUSMAN

STAR SONG SERIES

Published by Speaking Volumes

For more information
visit: www.SpeakingVolumes.us